Find Us In The Forest

J.R. Packard

Contents

Chapter 1
Escaping

A strange combination of fear, eagerness, and uncertainty struck the 17-year-old boy, Kyle's, mind, and in there dwelt the ponderance of being foreign. What that word meant–*foreign*–only he could speculate upon, but it was one of his favorites. In the bigger picture, he knew well what he wanted, but neither the smaller pieces of that dream nor the steps to make it manifest were present, as he sat at the classroom table and pretended to read a useless, meaningless book on a romance between two poor souls. The ideal romance in his eyes was the marriage between himself and the wild.

People, more than often, lie on their beds and doze off into another world where they experience fame or riches; few would imagine themselves entirely away from any worldly pleasures—even companionship. But it was, that Kyle did not like his life, nor civilization in general. Truth be told, there was little in his Washington town that he enjoyed, despite it being small and sleepy. As he'd walk home each day, like dull, uneventful clockwork, he'd feel an increasing sense of disdain towards the people about him and all of their messes. World War II had just passed and he could only imagine how long it'd be until another would break out and all that remained of the natural world was charred, wooden ash. Depressing, indeed. What was once a feeling of disheartment, eventually developed into anger with the greasy gangs outside deriding him on the streets.

He found solace in the works of Thoreau and Jack London. They understood life beyond speech and actions, knowing more the raw emotion one feels when seeing an innocent robin fly over a graceless, well-armed hunter. There was something about it; something attractive about living as a recluse and staying silent in a restless world. He too, like the former, was a poet, and was evermore getting skilled in attempting to put the natural world into words, while always keeping in mind that, in the end, it was impossible.

The kid did not have a dreadful nor unorthodox upbringing. As they should be, his parents were just as loving and caring as most, but he felt as though they incessantly–perhaps unintentionally–held him back from discovering his true self.

Such a thing was arguably common in the 1950's, with parents influencing their children's decisions in where they ought to live or work. His old man had fought on the battlefield and came home with severe shellshock, while, not being able to handle the pressure, his mother was on the verge of divorce. They fought frequently and ignored their only son most hours of the day. He was, in a sense, estranged to them, just like the rest of his peers and contemporaries. Not physically, but psychologically. They shared hardly anything in common; yet, notwithstanding this, he did, in fact, have loyal friends. They were few in number, but high in spirit and fidelity. Little did he know at the moment how vital they would be.

It may be said that the boy was in the wrong generation; instead being more rightly acquainted with paleolithic or antediluvian times when man was in its infancy. He did not belong in the institution known as a "town".

He continued to sit in his chair and stare at the clock above the door, while the other students did their actual duties. The plan was to go to Fairbanks. It was a city spot on in the center of high Northern Alaska: the most perfect of all foreign names: a land of milk and honey. In the vicinity of it was a small and lowly-populated area named "Bilorid". The masses would be oblivious to its existence, perhaps even native Alaskans, but it contained a may-as-well-be legendary waterfall which trickled down off an equally beautiful mountain. Kyle knew only of it from a travel magazine he'd received years prior.

It was nearing the end of October and, if they were to go, they knew it'd have to be soon. The other four who were planning on joining were seniors, as well, and, despite showing little in the way of care for it, they did not want to miss graduation. Obviously, it was an exceedingly naive thought. It would take three months at the least to make the over 2,000-mile trip there (let alone and back), given they did not hike the whole way. Even so, they were strong-willed and determined, despite young and suffering from ignorance. There was hope for completing high school, but it had no solid purpose in their eyes. Kyle was skeptical of his own plan.

There was no one reason for the trek. Part of it was to prove to himself that he was capable of undertaking the feat, and another was to immerse himself into the wilderness as much as possible. Yet, more than anything, it was for his best friend, Jordan.

Jordan wanted to see the far North more than anyone, and he was co-planner alongside Kyle. However, it was a hard pill for the latter boy to swallow, knowing that Jordan may not have survived the whole way in his condition. It was possible for him to recover from his horrendous ailment, but there were no definitives. Oddly, Jordan was the most pessimistic of recovery than any of their friends and family and, the way he wanted to leave the world, the proper way to die, was to see his dream come to fruition and pass in a land second to Heaven.

They equally wanted to escape the dissension of men–if only temporarily–and taste the wine of escapades. Kyle's favorite phrase, after all, was, "nothing ventured, nothing gained". It was a good idiom, he thought; the best of them, even. Truly, what was the purpose of living if one never knew a life of fun, the odor of fresh, piney air, or sight of majestic, unruly bears? It was a primal, instinctual intuition that had been lost, forgotten, and rejected. Sadly, he was aware that most preferred the comfort of tedious, meticulous, daily work, or the hypnosis of the unrealistic and fake radio and television.

Jordan had yet to be responding goodly to his therapies/treatments and he needed some semblance of happiness, at the very least. He, like Kyle, needed a type of escape, though in a slightly different way. Anything away would be better than staying at the frightening, painful hospital. In secret, Kyle didn't know how much time he had left and knew the diagnosis wasn't looking good. All he could do was comfort his friend, tell him it would all be alright, and make his final moments count–if they approached. He could only pray that he had the strength to make such an adventure.

"Alright, put your ridiculous book away." Said the teacher.

That's not really what she said, but what Kyle heard. He was more than happy to oblige.

She handed out their now-graded essays from the previous day. Kyle already knew he didn't do good. Were it a poem, he knew an easy A would be at the top, but in terms of all else, his interest was utterly absent. Social studies didn't matter. Math, history, science: all worthless, unneeded knowledge he'd never use when hiding out in his lost, remote cabin, feasting off the blossoms of foreign fruits.

Of course, he received an F. He couldn't help but half-chuckle inside, knowing that those around him assumed he was some sort of slacker, dumb in the mind, and as lazy as a turtle. No matter, he thought, the time was soon nearing when such letters would no longer follow him.

About four hours later, Kyle stood by the mirror in his room, slicked his hair with grease and combed it neatly to the side, making sure not to get any on his glasses. He was to attend the school's football game shortly thereafter, and it would likely be the last one. Curiously, unlike school, he enjoyed the games and was fond of competition. Mayhaps it was a reflection on the human/animal condition, where the fittest flourish, and nothing is stagnant, like sitting stale in a classroom. This is not taking into account the social nature of it, where he could freely hang out with his buddies without any peers looking down their shoulders and ruffling their hairs to stand on end via the breath. All kids alike came weekly.

He was met by his group standing outside, behind the bleachers smoking cigarettes in a circle. Kyle lit one up as he approached them.

"It's about time." Said Brandon. "Game's already nearly half-way through."

"Lay off, Brandon." Replied Erik. "When has he ever been on time with anything? At least he's here; we can't miss talking tonight."

The others in the group were Jordan and Dakoda (called, "Dak", for short). Jordan stood there fairly quiet as usual. He was arguably the

handsomest kid amongst them. What he made-up
for his small height was beautiful, blonde hair,
and brightly blue eyes. Kyle was perhaps second,
with fair skin, dark hair, and an intelligent face.
Jordan was the most innocent out of all of
them–perhaps even the school. He was
quick-witted like Kyle, but very humble and
possessing a golden heart. Indeed, he'd drop
anything on a whim to help another. The trip was
dedicated to him, and he more than deserved it.

Brandon was the polar opposite. The
tallest of the group, a tried-and-true greaser, and
perpetual sweater-wearer, he was their own
personal comedian and wildman. There was no
dare he'd back down from, nor fight he'd deny. It
was perhaps strange that he fit in with them so
closely, being different in personality and stature,
but, there was some unspeakable bond they had
all shared since grade school.

Meanwhile, Dak, was the complete obverse of him. He was not childlike, but neither accustomed to the *real*, adult world. He seemed to be scared of everything and had terrible anxiety. Around them, he was as outgoing as one can become, but elsewhere, as timid as a gopher. He went nowhere without his New York Giants' baseball cap, which he credited as a good luck charm. No one knew just how he'd survive after high school, and it was a complete enigma on why he considered going on the journey with them. It was well-known that he had the same emotional state as Kyle–longing for something outside of man's world, and the result of that world may have contributed to his nervous, avoidant character. Kyle hoped he'd grow out of it eventually, with the trip being that silver lining.

Lastly was Erik. He was the nerd of the group, which he compensated for by wearing white t-shirts, jeans, and a leather jacket.

Dissimilar to Kyle in this manner, he did want to graduate very passionately and admired school. However, he wished to go into the forest, not because of escape per se, but to learn. He desired to make the wilderness a new place of teaching and a home for his study. Both himself and Kyle were always on the same page when it came to loving the secrets of trees and mountains, rather than the mysteries of lackluster mathematics.

The boys had known each other since the fifth grade and were, for the most part, inseparable since. Again, it was an odd thing, seeing as they all had such different dispositions, but there was always one specific, important thing that forever held them together: loyalty. Originally, they were equal in the mannerisms that all young kids have, but naturally found their own differing paths with age; but the glue that bound their closeness together from so long ago never softened and they each admired their divergent feelings and interests. Perhaps that, indeed, is better than two people being precisely the same and becoming bored with one another. The adage was true: opposites attract.

As they made their way into the small stadium (if one could even call it that), they found a girl named Laura sitting above towards the top of the bleachers. The group had known her for a while and were friends, but not as much as Jordan, who always had a deep crush on her. They thought about sitting beside her in a fairly empty row, but made sure Jared, her boyfriend, wasn't with her.

Jared was a greaser like most, but an exceeding jerk who picked on and bullied any person with a sliver less of self-confidence than himself—which was, essentially, every person on the planet. Knowing Jordan's meek, lowly appearance and personality, he had always been a prime target—especially when rumor came out that he liked Laura. Being close to the rest, his friends were also extremely disliked by Jared and his gang, and would find themselves occasionally at heated knife-point; those situations never went anywhere, thankfully. None of them, and Kyle in particular, would let anything happen to Jordan and they stood up for him at every turn. He was the little, blameless brother of them.

The encounter was a conversation between the little brother and Laura, mostly, and, before they could sit down, the dreaded a-hole that was her boyfriend walked up the stairs from getting drinks below.

"What the hell are you doing?" He asked meanly, looking Jordan dead in the eyes.

"Leave him alone; he's just saying hi." Laura interjected.

"Get out of here—all of you—before I make you."

"Screw off, Jared." Said Brandon, the most outspoken of them. "We'll sit where we want."

Jared then reached into his pocket and quietly flipped open his switchblade, hiding it from other pedestrians.

"Whatever," said Kyle, "we were going anyway."

Encounters like that were frequent, and most more serious. They got off easy, and none of his "buddies" were with him to threaten additionally.

Jared and other similar students in the town's worst, most degraded school were by no means the single cause, but one of many bad factors that justified the boys' running away.

They went over to the other side of the field and watched on at the players, but sleet began to suddenly fall heavily, so they decided to leave as quickly as they came. No matter, they thought, they had more important matters to attend to. Crammed in Kyle's truck (he being the only kid to drive, oddly), they drove up to a mountainous area on the outskirts of the town. They're plans were not finalized and they had nowhere else to discuss it without either their parents or fellow students catching wind. They already had an excuse to be away from their folks. Besides, what better place to discuss the situation than in the woods itself?

At first, as they hung around near the car in a circle, chain smoked cigarettes, and drank rum and coke while listening to the baseball games, the conversation(s) was all jokes and stupid chit-chats. It wasn't after a half an hour that the topic on everyone's mind was finally brought up.

"I believe we should do it soon." Said Kyle.

"I agree." Responded Erik and Jordan.

"I'm thinking tomorrow."

"Good god, Kyle. At least another week." Said Erik.

"No, I agree with him." Jordan said confidently. "I can't bear staying here any longer."

Jordan was being honest, but not fully. He and Kyle knew it'd have to be as fast as possible, for Jordan was getting worse every day, unbeknownst to the others.

"We have to be on the same page right now—make a pact that we're all in this and won't back out." Jordan exclaimed calmly.

All but one nodded. Dak had continued to be on the fence about the trip since it was first proposed. Candidly, it wouldn't have mattered so much if it weren't for the fact that Dak was too much of a pansy. It wasn't out of the question that he'd let slip to someone out of pressure where the boys were headed to and for how long.

"Come on Dak." Kyle said. "Our whole world will change. Don't you want to experience something new: something actually good and away from this dump of a city and country?"

"What if we get lost? Or hurt? No one will ever find us. I don't want to be gone forever."

"We won't." Kyle responded. "It'll just be for a couple of months and there's five of us. We got each others' back."

"I'll let you know tomorrow; promise."

That was a good enough answer for the night.

"We'll head out tomorrow evening regardless." Said Kyle. "We'll have to leave the pick-up behind and lie in order to get out of the house. It'll be easily identified, and we won't have enough money for gas, anyways. Agreed?"

So they did.

The next hours were spent getting drunk and enjoying their remaining moments in civilization where they could live lavishly in a material world. As they continued in their stupor within the car for warmth, Brandon brought up a raw subject that was rarely talked about, and it was only because of the drink.

"Why did you never adopt him, Kyle?"

Of course, Brandon had only good intentions in mind, wanting Jordan to be happy and have a real home, but he must have known that, if it were feasible and Kyle had the means, he surely would have done that long ago.

The story of Jordan was a melancholic one. Yet young, he lived a life of forlornness, irrelevance, and despisement. It began the day he came into the world and it seemed that he never got any sort of reprieve, save when around Kyle.

His mother died while giving birth to him and, before then, his father was a very gentle and put-together man. After the incident, his old man couldn't cope. He was already nervous beforehand of raising a child and he could neither deal with the fact of doing that alone, nor moving on without his wife. He presumably tried his best for a few years, occasionally drinking his sorrows away. When Jordan was around 10, his dad quickly spiraled out of control with whiskey and abused Jordan on a daily basis. It was emotional and verbal at the start, but soon he came to school with purple bruises along his body and face. Child services eventually intervened (after calls from Kyle's parents) and the poor kid was placed in an orphanage, where he still remained. Kyle was as close to him as a brother and the truest family he had. He would have taken him in in an instant if he had a larger home. Notwithstanding all of that, his diagnosis came a month ago; right before adulthood. He deserved better. He deserved to see the grandest scenes and emotions Alaska and the North had to offer before the potentially inevitable would occur.

"Alright. I'll go." Dak suddenly spoke after a series of minutes staying quiet and thinking deeply.

"Hell yeah! We're really going to do this." Said Brandon.

"But if anything happens, anything at all, I'm heading straight back."

"You have my word, Dak." Said Kyle, holding out his hand.

The two shook each others' hands while Kyle attempted to hold back his glee. That was that. They'd leave the next day.

Chapter 2

The Leave

It was the following day when Kyle was in line in the school's cafeteria, eyeing the granola bars and shoving them vigorously into his pocket for the road. He then shuffled over to Jordan, who was sitting alone and not eating.

"You still haven't told them, have you?" He asked, while Kyle sat.

"About the cancer?"

"You have to promise to still keep it a secret. If the other guys find out, they won't go, let alone let me leave."

"You have my word, Jordan; but they may have to eventually find out. I don't like to say it, but you know you won't stay in this shape the whole way. They're going to think you have the flu, at the very least."

Jordan looked down at his fresh mashed potatoes, staring at them and trying to think.

"I know, you're right. I was the one who came up with this whole idea, but do you think this is the right decision? It's still possible I can be cured."

"It's up to you, buddy. Just say the word."

"I suppose it's too late to back out now." Said Jordan. "There's no place in a hundred miles that could cure me, and I don't want to die here in this town in some stupid orphanage. I want to go and spend the rest of what days I have left with you guys. I'm not spending the rest of my life in a hospital."

"Try to eat." Kyle said before Erik, Brandon, and Dak came with their food.

"So what's the verdict with time?" Asked Erik.

"I say we go at 4:00." Jordan responded. "Our folks will still be at work and sunset will settle in. We'll get as far as we can before it gets too dark."

"I agree." Said Kyle. "We'll meet up at Pete's Park on the edge of the valley, so leave right after school. We'll also all leave notes telling our parents that we're staying at each others' houses, so they won't suspect anything until tomorrow."

The rest of the boys nodded in agreement with nervous countenances. They were about to arguably make the biggest decision of their lives—one that could even end with their deaths or arrests. Both outcomes were exceedingly unlikely, but the possibility remained, and no one knew quite what to expect. Kyle was the only kid with a proper amount of experience in the wild, and he'd inevitably have to be the guiding force. Even he was unsure of his abilities in the deep unknown and unexplored.

Kyle quickly ran his bike home the second the final bell rang. He had little time to get his affairs in order before his parents returned. The others were conceivably dependent on him most, and he couldn't afford to be late.

The first thing to do was take his father's old military backpack. It provided a good amount of room, was comfortable, and extremely sturdy. He hoped to take a gun of any caliber along, but his father, in his paranoid and jumpy condition, had sold them off years before.

Having earned the rank of Eagle in the BSA, he was quite knowledgeable of necessities to gather; yet that did little to stop him from bringing two full cartoons of cherished menthol cigarettes.

The pack was filled to the brim: 12 cans of miscellaneous soups/chillies/meats, packets of jerky, two jars of peanut butter, a canteen, a woolen blanket, knives, matches, three small emergency blankets, a portable shovel, a miniature hatchet, a first aid kit, and lightweight winter wear. All-in-all, the poundage came out to be about 50. It'd surely be a strain, but would make him stronger. Lastly, he managed to stuff the treasured Call of the Wild in–his all time favorite book.

He was about to leave before remembering to write a note. He paused for a few moments, contemplating on what he'd put on it. He wanted his parents to worry as little as possible, but also had to be cautious in not giving away where precisely they were headed to. Ultimately, he stated that he loved them dearly, was not doing anything dangerous (a lie) or illegal, and promised to be back in a few month's time. The note was attached to the front of the fridge, he took a good, final look around the house, and opened the door, never to look back until his mission was fulfilled.

Kyle hopped on his bike, finding out a mile in that riding it would prove impossible with the sheer weight of his belongings. He chose to strap the pack onto it, and walk alongside it. About an hour later–5:00 PM, to be specific, he reached the park and found the rest of the boys there, waiting impatiently for him.

Before departing, they looked over and examined what everyone brought. It was all about the same as Kyle's luggage, but they were interested in Brandon, who had taken his pellet gun with him. Surely, a real gun would have been more useful, but his was powerful and could take down small game with ease, like rabbits and squirrels; better than nothing. Erik put forward a radio and map. The rest were embarrassed for forgetting such dire pieces of survival.

Not far from them was a very large hill that divided the mountains from the valleys below. Beside the park, was a small cafe where they stopped to have coffee and ice cream: the final delicacies before months of bland, unseasoned meat and wild vegetables. Total, it cost them about $2, and $15 remained. They had no idea when that money would come to use, but nevertheless well to have on-hand.

Two miles came to pass, while hiking along switchbacks, when they finally reached the peak. Half way up, they finally ditched the bike, which proved to be far too cumbersome.

They all turned to look at the city below, reddened by the sun setting. It at last completely dawned on them that there was no turning back. What they were doing was the real deal, and they'd have to persevere. All that could get in their way was Dak, who'd force them to leave at the sight of merely a coyote; but that concern was for another time.

Directly further down the trail, was a couple of apple orchards that sat beside the mountains. Seeing as it was getting dark at a fast rate, they decided to camp inside one and await the morning before doing the arduous task of climbing. They had to ensure they remained hidden from the owners and farmhands, but it hardly mattered under the veil of nighttime.

About that time, the coldness of the Fall began to set it, and they hoped to make their first fire. Ironically, despite being the 50s, where it should have been common knowledge, Kyle was the only boy privy to making one. He wasn't keen on the idea–fearing it'd attract too much attention, but after continual hassles by the others, he finally relented and made a small one with the tepee method, wherefore they all cheered.

While talking beneath the stars about the philosophies of girls, dread of school, and cars, Erik and Brandon got the bright idea to make spears. Kyle thought it was fairly ridiculous, seeing that, if they truly ended up needing them, it'd be far down the road when their food ran out, but, nonetheless, if they wanted to act primitive and get in the mindset of the ancients, then Kyle was more than pleased with it. They'd end up, over an hour, chasing birds and rodents bent on stealing fruit. Of course, they failed at every instance.

Bandon was certainly the most adventurous and feral of the group, with Erik following closely behind him. Both had no issue being upfront, brutally honest, and outspoken. They had no sense of shame, embarrassment, nor humiliation. They lived their lives as they chose to, and there were few people in the world that'd get in the way of that. They both (but Brandon, especially), possessed unconventional, uncivilized ideas that didn't align with their given generation, and Kyle was exceedingly admirable of it.

They all ended up passing out around the warm flames and awoke in the morning to find the fire only smoldering coals, yet still giving off plumes of smoke. Jordan, the first to get up, quickly exclaimed for the others to do the same and put it out. Surely, and most certainly, the owner would see the blackened air rising over the trees. Not wishing to waste any of their precious water, he convinced them to all urinate on it, which they did with competition.

"Alright, we need to head out." Said Kyle.

They took advantage of the endless apples around them, and gathered up as much as they could muster when, out of nowhere, from an unknown direction, came the sound of shouting and a gunshot. Immediately and without hesitation, the boys ran to their packs.

"Get the hell out of my orchard!" Yelled a man in the distance, running after them.

Again, the gun rang off. It was likely only a cherry one to scare off birds, but they were taking no chances. They sprinted as fast as they could until they disappeared into the treeline, whereupon the man lost them, looked attentively for a moment, and turned around.

They couldn't help but laugh as they caught their breaths. It was the first thrill of their thriller story. It got their adrenaline pumping, and they were eager for it to happen again–save Dak, who fervently berated their stupidity.

"Lighten up, Dak." Said Jordan. "He wasn't going to do anything."

"You guys are idiots." Replied Dak, but not able to hold back a smile. Deep down, he liked his new experience, and breaking out of his comfort zone. "I guess it beats studying all day."

"Damn right." Said Kyle.

From that point onwards, they'd head East, and would soon find themselves in desert country after the mountain; it'd remain that way until the Washington-Idaho border.

They quickly realized the tedium of the mountain was more than they imagined, and it'd only get harder. Thankfully, they had the divine intervention of a trail, but it'd soon end, and they'd have to have their wits about them if they hoped to continue in the right direction or suffer the thick brambles of forests.

Hours passed when, at last, they reached the top, falling down on their backpacks out of exhaustion. They got to their feet minutes later and saw a vast view of the desert-ish central Washington awaiting them below. It stretched beyond the horizon, and over a hundred miles lay ahead.

"Can we just stop here for the night?" Asked Dak, lying back-first on his backpack.

"We can't." Replied Jordan. "We've covered only three miles so far. At this rate, it'll take years to get to Alaska. We need to cover at least 20."

Both he and Brandon couldn't help but groan.

"How are we going to do this?" Said Brandon, slightly joking. "I wasn't expecting it to be this hard."

"The desert will be easy. It's cool this time of year and fairly flat. We'll get our legs in shape 'til we encounter mountains again."

After 30 minutes of snacking on Jerky and relaxing, they decided to descend. They encountered the bottom a few hours later at about 3:45.

"Come on, Kyle. Let's make camp." Said Dak.

Kyle was noticeably irritated. They had covered only six miles since the morning and they'd have to do far better. It was unacceptable to cover such mileage: not bad, necessarily, for six is a well worth number, but if they ever hoped to get anywhere, they'd have to step up.

"It's up to Jordan." He said.

The innocent boy thought for some seconds—he being just as worn out.

"I say we stay, but tomorrow has to be better."

Kyle couldn't argue with him. He'd never go against Jordan's wishes—especially given his illness and the whole trip dedicated to him. If Jordan wanted to rest, then he deserved to rest.

After setting up the tents, they relaxed the remainder of the day, and for the most part, did their own things. Dak and Jordan sat around the radio, listening to a baseball game, while Brandon and Erik took naps.

Kyle couldn't help but simply stare into the distance and chain smoke cigarettes with his notepad on his lap. He was far past content, feeling enormous peace in the silence and solace of the remote. There was no bona fide citizen to interrupt his thoughts, nor teacher to dictate what he should think. No, he was with the people he'd take over any and bask in the noble, graceful light that the sun emitted unto his already dirty face.

He considered composing a poem at that moment—a desire he felt a great sense of pride in.

Though, for an undefined reason, he stopped himself. He considered that some experiences and feelings are left better untold and unspoken. Indeed, he thought, most are worthy of sharing, but some, however few, are simply too powerful and moving to put into English, and that was a good thing. He wanted to enjoy the divine scene in the moment and not soil it with the opinions of others; photography was similar.

For a while, he'd been dwelling on the thought of writing a book of poetry and potentially getting it published. Even so, he doubted his abilities and the aforementioned mindset somewhat got in the way of it. Above all, the poems were for himself and he'd be pleased to look back on them once they returned from their pilgrimage.

His faith in humanity was utterly lost in the fiery, spikey world, and, there was even a small portion of his being that considered man didn't deserve to experience such wondrous, foreign words he'd jot down. The wild possums; the magnificent Douglas Firs; the expanse of unexplored terrain: all things that deserve to be seen, smelled, tasted, and heard in person. The layman, too preoccupied by his wealth and suffocating livelihood, would never seek it out.

Jordan was the complete opposite in that regard, but Kyle would never contradict or argue with him. He loved humanity, wishing them the best and forever entrusting his faith that they could do good if they only attempted. He simply had the inclination to feel what a world outside of them was like. Indeed, he had faith in nearly everything and saw the positive forces of existence when Kyle saw but pessimism. He relished the small things with a strong appreciation. It all became evermore sad and unfortunate then, that in spite of those beautiful outlooks, he had a terrible life. He didn't deserve it, and Kyle cursed the firmament in retaliation, but tried to use Jordan's logic that there was something out there tending life and everything would inevitably be okay.

Kyle contemplated if it was all right; in that moment, that is. Was it a correct decision to bring Jordan along? Would he make it to the end? Would they return, Jordan be cured, and live their lives for a proper, fair while? He could only use Jordan's hope.

Chapter 3
A Good Couple

Kyle's mother didn't know what to think as she stared down at his note while eating breakfast. His parents, albeit draining, were not overly emotional, nor irrational by any means. At first notice of his disappearance, she didn't cry or break down, but her limbs grew heavy with worry and concern.

"He'll be back, Jane." Kyle's father said, sitting across from her while sipping coffee. "He's a big boy and won't get into serious trouble. Relax."

Anyone ought to have known that recommending a mother to "relax" when her child had just mysteriously gone and left was not the best decision; yet a part of her was in agreement. She knew Kyle could handle himself in the most grave of situations and he almost certainly wasn't breaking the law. Nevertheless, she rarely lingered out of the room with their phone on the chance that she'd inform the police. The only thing stopping her was her husband, who acted as though she was being dramatic for even having the thought of something being wrong. It was by no means uncommon for Kyle and his pals to stay up late and bounce around the town, but he'd always return by morning and never left such a cryptic note. She continued to wait.

Little had she known just how ambitious her son was becoming at that exact hour.

It was the first day in the desert and the boys, oddly, were more attracted to it than the previous day's trailing of the mountain. The ground was dusty, but stable and easily walkable—as opposed to the rocky, uneven surfaces before.

Kyle had been in the setting numerous times whilst in Boy Scouts, but never at that time of year. In some ways, he loved and loathed it; by that, meaning he loved the sagebrush, dryness, and expanse, but hated the scorching heat it could impose. To him at that moment, however, it was unconditionally perfect. The temperature was likely around forty, which, combined with the additional heat created by walking/hiking, felt substantially amazing.

Earlier that morning, before they forsook camp, they cooked canned chili and Brandon got the bright idea of seasoning it with wild sagebrush. Unbeknownst to all of them, desert sagebrush is not cooking sage. As they shared the can, their stomachs turned sour, and the whole lot of them vomited at least once, coming to learn their first lesson: don't eat what you don't know. Of anyone, Kyle should have known better, and felt a sense of stupidity. It made him consider–even by that simple, inconspicuous act–that he didn't know nearly as much as he thought he did about the wild.

The others were in a surprisingly cheerful mood from the second they started. They presumably slept well the night prior out of tiredness, and were fueled by the idea of already abandoning humanity–ready to push the limits of just how far away they could go. It made both Jordan and Kyle happy, now having the others share the anticipation the two had had since the beginning.

Truth be told, they were finally having fun, which mattered most. They'd race and kick dirt at one another, with Jordan being the most enthusiastic participant. Brandon held onto his hallowed spear tightly as he walked, prepared to strike any rattlesnake or mini scorpion they could wander upon.

There was little in the land, save the occasional sighting of coyotes in the far distance or filthy hares jumping around, and that's the way Kyle liked it. He admired the changes the foreign country went through in even a day: vast layers of frost in the morning, sun during the day with creeping critters emerging, and light rain and wind in the evening. The five of them were their own puny civilization of sorts amidst it; no, more properly, an unmanaged pack or herd unfettered by the iron grip of man's laws and norms.

For the first time, Kyle was beginning to experience the pain of adventure. His legs were well-oiled and made of steel, but, like Dak and Jordan, his feet were in the process of blistering and each step was a burning one. In addition, his mangey, old boots which he got when he was 14, were squeezing something fierce and slowly splitting at the seams. He was forced to wrap duct tape around them to even keep them in one piece; it did not help the smothering.

Focusing on inner thoughts while trying to get his mind off of the pain, he took seriously what his parents were doing and how they felt. Surely, by then they had known something was wrong, and he wished they truly knew he'd make a safe return. He detested that he brought them some form of alarm–maybe even sorrow–but, in his mind, was forced to. To him, he was doing something monumental for his being and he could wait no longer to spread his wings. Every day he grew older equated to every day growing depressed. Every person has their limits to what they can endure. His tolerance for the ordinary was long ago exceeded.

Around 1:00, they neared running out of water; it was not great planning on the part of any of them. Still, they had already accomplished eight miles, and their pace was increasing exponentially compared to the previous day.

Looking on the map, they could see countless small ponds and lakes spread sporadically across the barren landscape, but, with no real checkpoints to gauge where exactly they were, they knew it'd be a dangerous (and frankly, stupid) choice to continue blindly. A meek highway ran straight about a half mile from them and Kyle took it to a vote on if they should hitchhike. Oddly, most of the boys were against it, and not for the reason of getting caught. They had set their eyes on testing themselves and didn't want to succumb to the mercy of others. It was a noble trait, but living was of higher importance, and water was the ultimate factor.

Kyle was the most fervent and hell-bent against catching a ride, but he couldn't deny the circumstance either. A cool, fresh, and crisp lake could have been on the other side of a hill, at best; 50 miles away, at worst. It was likely that he'd take the risk, were it just him, but he couldn't gamble the souls of the rest–especially not Jordan, who'd need the droplets most to keep his failing pancreas painless.

They decided to take a vote on it. After arguing where they were on the map and whether they'd get caught, Brandon (of all people), took the stand and demanded they get a ride, telling them that it'd be stupid to wander. For once, he seemed to have given thought in what he was doing and acted smart. He managed, quite successfully with his charisma, to persuade the others, and they made a sharp right towards the highway.

As they approached it, Erik and Brandon folded their shirts in makeshift handkerchiefs and tied them around their mouths.

"You guys really think that'll do anything?" Scoffed Kyle.

"Better safe than sorry."

"We fit the description of five lost boys our age." Said Jordan. "I don't think covering half of our faces is going to hide our identities."

Whatever, thought Kyle. If it eased their minds, then let them do it.

Earning a ride was far more difficult than they imagined. About three cars passed them per hour, and none would bother to stop. Indeed, they were in the middle of nowhere, and the highway was still young. Eventually, thirst and dried, cracked lips got the best of them, and they could no longer walk. They chose to rest beside the road, take their shirts off, and make a canopy with an emergency blanket. All they could do was hope, not drink their last sips of water, and wait. It was only the second day, and already, they were facing fear of the worse. Surely, they wouldn't die, but the frit thought that no one would ever come or stop was ever present.

At last, by the grace of the foreign and virgin badland, a red 1949 Ford f-3 truck came along three hours later and slowed before stopping beside them.

"Where' you boys headed to?" Asked an older man in the driver's seat.

"Water, sir. Somewhere with lots of water."

"Water? What on Earth are you even out here for with no vehicle?" The ol' man looked around at the dehydrated boys staring at him with pitiful faces.

"Drifters?"

"Something like that." Kyle replied.

"How 'bout you come back with me. I have a farm. Work a little for me and I'll give you some change and a good meal."

Kyle looked behind them to see the expressions of the rest. They all looked pleased at the offer and he had to respect democracy.

"Thank you, sir. We'll take it."

The boys quickly scrambled their belongings together and hopped in the bed, while Kyle got in the passenger's seat.

"I'm George." Said the man. "You're runaways, aren't ya?"

"You're not going to say anything ar–"

"Crap, kid. I'm not turning you in. I ran away plenty when I was your age. Pretty damn stupid to be out here of all places, though."

Kyle wasn't against the idea of doing an odd job for some spare change but, as before, he didn't want to stay long. Finally, they were beginning to make good time, and they couldn't become veal in the pin of the farmer's house. Tired and weak with inner drought, he quickly fell asleep.

He awoke to find them at a small homestead in-between a steppe climate and woods, while the boys jumped out the back. As George went to the door, the others noticed the well spout and ran to it, ferociously dowsing their faces beneath the running water.

"You could've come in for that." Said the man.

He led them to the barn where he showed them the tractor.

"Move the hay bales into here, and you two come with me." He said, pointing at Jordan and Kyle.

He took the two behind the house and asked them to pick vegetables and fruits, before going inside.

It was fairly easy work, and the two kids were quite happy to eat the berries and string beans while they worked. It was the first time either of them actually did real (or semi-real) work for money, instead of mowing their own lawns or weeding for their folks.

"How are you feeling, Jordan?"

"My stomach hurts, but it's bearable; I just hope it stays this way as long as it can."

Kyle commented on how good he looked–which wasn't a lie. He comforted him that it'd all work out and they'd come back changed people for the better. Jordan didn't need such gentle words. He knew full well what he wanted and, one way or another, was determined to make it to Alaska. The ludicrous notion of cancer wouldn't get in the way of it.

As they talked, they both subtly filled their pockets with the beans and baby potatoes. He wouldn't have missed a couple, they thought.

It was in the evening when George came back out and applauded their work, saying they could stop. His misses had made supper, and they were more than welcome to eat with their pay. They had only been missing a few days, but an extravagant ham feast meant the world, having merely subsisted off of canned food during that duration.

They made good conversation while sipping coke, but were careful not to give away too much of their plan or origin. George had taken notice of Kyle's shoes and gave him a pair of his own afterward. He, too, had fought in the war, and both the boots and long knife he generously handed him were from the front. One may assume he didn't want any memorabilia that would remind him of it.

The man proposed they stayed the night, which they considered with interest, but ultimately decided against. It was about 6:00 PM, but he surprisingly further offered to drive them all the way to the next town on the other side of the Idahoan border—a good four hour drive. They couldn't help but accept. It was dually a good plan, as the Washington police weren't likely communicating with them. And any way to get farther, the better.

Chapter 4

A Lonely Meal

Kyle's dad stared down at the cash register, forlorn and contemplating with a blank visage. For the first time, after the passing of several days, he started to seriously think deeply of Kyle and his friends. The customers would continually check out their items, and, despite being the manager who'd always be the most jubilant in greeting respectable taxpayers, he stood there, fairly silent and even scared. His past scoffing at the idea that there was anything wrong had diminished. He dearly loved his son, but took into consideration that he'd been distancing himself from him over the past year. Indeed, if Kyle did run away, he thought, he couldn't help but finally blame himself, even if moderately. His utter fear was that something terrible had happened to his boy; he shunned that thought immediately. Most of all, he regretted not telling him just how proud he was.

Coincidently, Erik's parents happened to walk in that day for milk and bread. Seeing as the boys were all extraordinarily close to one another, right at the hip, and were all equally friends with each other's folks, Erik's parents suspected that Kyle was missing as well.

At checkout, they brought up the subject. Holding up the line with irritated customers, they could only share in their own confusions and inquire if the other had any useful knowledge. Both were equivalently speechless and desperate for information.

Feeling sympathy for the couple, the father proposed they join him for dinner that night—maybe hoping to solve the case. They obliged, having nowhere else to turn to, save the useless, small police force with no wherewithal, who'd only searched the city at their behest and nowhere else.

It was later that night when they sat at the dinner table. There was no formal (or informal) greetings at the door; rather, lonesome and perturbed silence, which was honestly expected. This remained, even as the couple sat at the table and downed coffee. It wasn't until the meals were served when chatting truly began.

It was related to Kyle's parents that, apparently, the family of Erik had known that Brandon, Jordan, and Dak were also elsewhere. This fact brought only more suspicion and conjecture.

Oddly, this was mildly comforting. If it were only one of the boys, foul play—as horrible as it sounded—may have been on the table; but with five able-bodied young adults, there was little question that that was not nearly the case. Incidentally, it just so happened to be laid out that the boys *did* run away. It was plausible, but didn't hold up to scrutiny in their eyes. To all of them (besides Kyle's dad's recent doubt), they believed they were the best of parents and could see no reason for it. If only they knew the greatest purpose had nothing to do with them, and they were but small factors.

There was much ground to believe Jordan's rationale for escaping his life, but they would never in a million years consider just how truthful it was that he was the ringleader. His cancer casted the most uncertainty and frankly, they must have all worried the most for him besides their own kin.

None of their theories utterly made sense to them. Brandon had ambitions to attend college following graduation, and both families believed their children were too smart to leave. Any of them had more than enough credentials to get into a university of their choosing. Why would they seemingly throw their lives away? All they could do was wait. All they could do was pin their hopes on the teens' safety. Hardly would they have guessed that the runaways were living more than them and experiencing the human condition in all its primordial, ancestral, and natural aspects.

Chapter 5

The First Fear

The boys had awoken in the back of the Ford around midnight. It was difficult to tell where they were in the blackness, but the tender light of the full moon bathed the landscape and reflected off the swaths of trees. He apologized for dropping them off there instead of a city, as he had promised. It would have been another hour's drive, which stretched the strength of the old man, who'd already stayed up far past his bedtime. Even so, the boys were more than thankful. They had at last made it to Idaho and were left beside an unknown trail that led to God knows where.

As he drove off, they were left there: in the middle of the eerily silent, dark forest with only one flashlight lit to conserve batteries.

Hastedly, and still in a sleepy daze, they set up a tent beside the road. At this point, still mere boys, they feared sleeping outside with their sleeping bags. None would say it, but they were all moderately scared, besides Kyle who was used to the setting. True, the forest can be a hair-raising place at midnight. Feeling their unease, he volunteered to stay up and keep watch in the tent until daybreak. They pretended to act indifferent to the suggestion, but did not object.

While sitting within it, arms over knees, and listening to the annoying, incessant snoring of Dak, Kyle felt a sense of warmth and composure. He was already changing and believed the others were, as well, though in the smallest amount. He was taught and raised to be domesticated, but gradually undoing himself and returning to nonexistent roots; it was what he was meant for. Though, in him, was still a sense of fear: the stirring and agitation of the *foreign*. Boy

Scouts was not close to being as immersive within the woods as he was then. He was accustomed to being a recluse and a stranger to cities, but the city and civilization was still ingrained in him–however little. They all–including himself–would have to grow much stronger and hardened if they hoped to continue. Unintentionally, he slowly dozed off to sleep, meaning to rest his eyes.

He was suddenly jolted by Dak tugging at his arm.

"Do you hear that?" He whispered.

There were loud howlings of wolves both in the distance and what appeared to also be near the tent. The others soon awoke via the commotion.

"Calm down." Said Kyle.

"They could attack us. Turn on the flashlight!" Dak exclaimed.

"For God sakes, Dak. Relax. They won't bother with us; not in a tent."

"You were supposed to stay up.--" Said Brandon in a somewhat angry tone.

"It's fine guys." Jordan interrupted, rubbing one of his eyes. "This is the woods. Get used to it."

"Well I'm not going back to sleep."

"Me neither." Said Erik and Dak.

Kyle could only shake his head and chuckle inside at their ridiculousness. He thought about jump-scaring them, but ultimately decided against it, not wanting to be punched.

They found themselves escaping from the tent in the morning to walk on thick, frosty grass and frozen twigs. They did indeed stay up all night and wished to rest through the day, though knew they couldn't. Finally, they were where they wanted to be. The desert was hard, sure, but it lasted only a day. Now they were in the jarring, hardy country and it'd get more difficult the deeper they went. Snow would soon fall and many plants would wither the higher they'd go.

Kyle huddled around Jordan and looked back-and-forth between the map and trail head. After walking a ways down the road and finding its number, they deduced which trail it was and found that it went North: exactly what they were hoping for. It stopped and turned away right before the Canadian border, so they'd have to power through the rough, ungodly terrain. It excited the two best friends.

As Kyle glanced upwards at his friend, his heart sank a little. Jordan did not look well that morning. He was pale–more than he should've been, even in the cold, and showed signs of light jaundice in his eyes.

"Have you been eating, pal?" He asked Jordan.

"I haven't been feeling like it."

Kyle demanded that he should and went over to get him some canned meat. His worry immediately turned to anger when he found five cans missing.

"Did you guys move food?" He asked the group.

Erik, Jordan, and Dak gave a "no" at the same time, but Brandon stood silent, for which they all looked at him.

"Was it you who ate more?" Dak asked.

"Look, I was hungry. I'm bigger than the rest of you; I need more rations."

"What the hell, Brandon!" Yelled Erik.

The other boys, meanwhile, stood up and paced out of vexation.

"You idiot!" Said Dak. "It's not all about you. Are you going to be the one that does the hunting?"

"Relax, okay?" Said Brandon, calmly and looking guilty. "I will do the hunting. I'll catch us a deer and we'll be fed for a week."

"What, with your stupid spear?" Replied Dak.

"Yes."

The others shook their heads out of frustration.

"It's fine." Said Jordan. "For now on, we keep each other in check. If someone takes more than their fair share, they don't eat for a day."

They nodded.

"I'm sorry, guys." Said Brandon. "'Won't do it again. Promise."

He tried to shake Jordan's hand. Jordan gave a deep sigh but accepted his apology and took his hand.

Kyle went over to get a remaining can (which was supposed to be his personal ration for the day) and tried to give it to Jordan in private.

"Here. You need it more."

"I can't, Kyle. I'll probably throw up anyway."

"Don't make me force you, man." Said Kyle with the smallest grin.

Twenty minutes later, they were all packed up, having oddly never made a fire. They stood together, looking onward at the trail that disappeared aways into the treeline.

"Alright," Said Kyle. "Let's get to Alaska."

Chapter 6

A Dangerous Situation

The day kicked off well. Shortly following their departure down the evenly-graded and little-used trail, the sun arose with a gentle, kindly softness, swiftly melting the sea of frost away. They were utterly surrounded by mighty, sprawling trees, and there was no way to tell what part of the forest they were in, nor what awaited them around each bend: features and mysteries Kyle was very fond of.

Erik attempted to use his radio for music, but found that it obviously didn't have reception. In lieu, he attempted to start singing himself, but was quickly shut down by others. They agreed on creating riddles for each other, and assigned chores for the losers to pass the time away. Four hours later, when boredom and fatigue were reaching a peak, the rest gave in and sang the Big Rock Candy Mountain together.

It was Kyle's word that they walked along the ravines between the mountains/hills–generally beside a stream or river, even if there was no trail. They saw that an unknown river they were following led North in a straighter path than the designated trail. Just as well, the animal-made paths tended to go up and over mountains and distanced them from treasured water.

A total of 13 miles into the day, they came upon a small pond that was loosely connected to the river. Feeling that their efforts could be rewarded, they stopped for a deserved rest and bath in the water.

The boys were more than pleased to jump to stop and instantly brought out some food.

Given their way, they'd eat at every chance they could.

"I have an idea." Said Kyle with a cigarette in his mouth, looking at the river. "What if we stayed here for a couple of days? We could build canoes and glide up into Canada. 'Save us a lot of time."

"How are we going to do that?" Asked Dak.

"We'll do it like the Indians did—get a tree trunk and burn the inside out of it."

They were all noticeably excited at the idea. It'd mean less walking, faster travel, and most importantly—fun.

Brandon convinced them all to go swimming after eating. The wilderness had fooled them. They were hot from hiking, but it was 40 degrees out, giving the impression that the water would feel good. In an instant, they raced over to a large boulder while throwing their shirts off, where they'd jump at the same time.

About a third of a second after hitting the water, they regretted their decision. They all couldn't help but exclaim swear words at the chilling pond, until their bodies half-way acclimated to it.

It seemed almost a right-of-passage, to Kyle, but so was nearly everything they did. Immersing himself in an ungodly, unsympathetic, piercing water felt like some sort of primeval baptism. The climate there in that season was not for the faint-hearted survivalists. It was far and removed from man's country.

As they splashed water on one another, Kyle took a glance at their campsite and had to rub the water from his eyes for a better look.

"Well, that's unfortunate." He said.

They looked to see a family of black bears rummaging through their packs for food.

"Dammit Erik! I told you to tie the food in the trees." Said Brandon.

Like a wild man with dementia, he frantically began yelling at the bears to scare them off, which surprisingly seemed to work. It was indeed a humorous sight—someone getting incredibly worked up (perhaps even scared) over a meager, innocent black bear.

They mocked and dared one another with how long each could last. Dak was the first to drop out, of course, with Jordan second. Kyle desperately wanted to win and prove himself to be the hardiest out of them, but quickly swam to shore after, along with Erik, leaving Brandon as the champion of the frigid.

Thankfully, Jordan took the initiative in starting a fire beforehand, and they had little trouble warming up. Once settled, they went straight to work with the canoes–not wanting to needlessly waste any time.

First thing to do was make the fire as big as possible, so they had a fresh, substantial supply of coals. Brandon, being the strongest, was delegated with the task of cutting thick logs and rolling them near. All-in-all, getting everything ready took about four hours. They cut the tops of the logs flat and shoveled the scorching coals on top to be left overnight.

They spent the remainder of the night huddled around the fire, sitting on logs: their daily, yet never lacking, routine. The number one thing on everyone's mind was food. They were running low on it, and starving to begin with, with only eating around a thousand calories per day each. They anticipated hunting soon, and trying their hands in fishing.

It was around midnight when everyone was sound asleep in the tent, save Jordan and Kyle, still burning their fixed eyes at the divine, immaculate fire. Jordan had been whittling away at a piece of antler he found earlier that day while on the trail. He seemed to have been agitated the whole night, like something was all of the sudden eating away at him. He was less talkative, and when he did speak, it was faint and subdued sounding. After Kyle finally brought it up, he seemed relieved to get his thoughts off his chest.

Jordan related that he was, very much, happy where they were and what they were doing, but was becoming bitter about the cancer and didn't like it. As much as he'd always had faith and hope, he couldn't help but start thinking life was unfair. For once, he was angry at his illness, rather than sad, and couldn't wrap his mind around *why him*. He never showed his discontent through all the trials he endured growing up, but it seemed to have come to the surface at that moment. Perhaps it was the volatile, strong, and intense emotions that arose once they left. It was something none of them had imagined they'd do; neither did Jordan, especially, given his condition. As much as he loved what he was doing, the stress was creeping up on him. Kyle more than understood, but wished he could relate more. He couldn't begin to imagine how Jordan must've felt, and truly wasn't even told much, despite their relationship. He knew deep down that Jordan was cognizant, at least a little, of his potential death. It must have been awful.

Kyle felt useless and helpless, wishing he could do something, but lady fate was the ultimate, deciding judge of what would become of Jordan; all he could do was be there for him.

"Here." Said Jordan, handing Kyle the antle. "It's a whistle. Good to have for emergencies."

Kyle was touched by the gift and hoped to make him something in turn down the road.

"Don't worry, man. You'll get better, promise. These next days will be easy—no walking and we'll get some good food."

Jordan said little, took a relieving sigh, and lay down beside the fire in his sleeping bag.

"Goodnight, man." He said.

Kyle opened his eyes in the cold morning to the sight of Brandon doing something beside a tree.

"What are you doing?"

"Making a water filter." He said. "Read it in a survival book before we left."

Kyle arose and inspected it. He'd heard about such an apparatus–one to filter water via gravity through charcoal and sand.

Brandon poured a jug of water into it, stuck his head underneath, only for his face to be covered in black, sluggish liquid.

"Ew." Said Dak. "What's in there?"

"Sediment from the lake. It's how you're supposed to do it."

"Gross." Replied Kyle. "Better to just drink the river water."

"More for me." Said Brandon, sticking his head underneath again for more gulps, explaining that it was "organic".

The other guys went straightaway to making another fire and finishing the canoes. It was tedious work, burning and scraping out the charred wood over and over again, but they did, most certainly, make progress.

They ended up carving three total: one for Erik and Dak (who was too scared to go by himself), another for Brandon and Jordan, and the last for Kyle. Making paddles was the easy part, and each had their own. At about 3:00 PM, they were ready.

Truth be told, as excited as they were, Dak was not the only one nervous. They were good swimmers and the river was exceedingly calm, but no one knew how it'd be 50 miles downstream. They considered tying the vessels together, but ultimately decided against it, fearing that, due to their weight, if one went down, so would the rest. They had to stay close, no matter what. They did, however, tether their backpacks and belongings to themselves. If those were lost, their situation would be far more dire.

Together, they placed their canoes on the bank, and had one person from each ready to push off. In an instant, they were successfully in the water, side-by-side, and sailed smoothly.

They cheered as they calmly drifted along the relaxed, unruffled river as their archaic, venturous ancestors, Lewis and Clark, did. They moved relatively slow, but greatly quicker than if they were walking.

Oddly, they managed to float for days on end, each taking turns sleeping. It was very dangerous continuing at night, and it was extremely foolish, but they had yet to learn that. There were the occasional moments of rushing streams (during the day, thankfully) but, for the most part, it remained the same, and they'd have it no other way. Water was plentiful to drink, but the food on every boat had essentially run out. No matter; they wanted to keep the pace up, and the day came when they were prepared to temporarily land.

The sun arose and making land was planned in a few hours. Then it happened.

They noticed the river was increasing in speed, but nothing to be too alarmed about. Yet, as they came around a corner, they saw a terrible turbulence. About 300 feet in the distance, the water spread and shallowed out, revealing violent, white waves crashing against boulders. Without an ounce of thinking, they screamed at one another to row to the banks–which were fortunately lowly fields of small rocks.

Suddenly, they began to feel the boulders beneath them kiss their wooden trunks. One after another, they all capsized, and desperately tried to swim with all their might, struggling with the weight of their backpacks trying to hold them down. Meanwhile, their canoes jolted into the endless rocks and flew into the air in all directions. The worst was to come–the part where they'd surely be torn to pieces and have no hope of coming to shore. They had to act fast.

Kyle, Brandon, Dak, and Erik managed to exhaustedly drag themselves onto the heaven that was the field of flat rocks, but Jordan, with his small frame, was still floating and yelling with all his might.

Each of the boys rapidly tore off their packs and grabbed long, fresh twigs or slender longs, running alongside the river and holding them out for Jordan. Be it perhaps by divine intervention, Jordan managed to get a grasp of one and was pulled in before he approached sure death 50 feet away.

As he got to his feet, the boys' enervation quickly turned to anger towards Kyle for creating the idea in the first place.

"Asshole!" Yelled Dak. "This is your fault!--"

"Yeah." Said Erik.

"How was I supposed to know this?" Kyle responded, attempting to defend himself. "And you all agreed with me that it was a good idea. Don't tell me I forced you."

"Shut up!" Said Jordan, catching his breath. "It's no one's fault; we all agreed on it."

"This is it. I want to go home." Said Dak.

"Don't be ridiculous."

"We could've died, Jordan. I told you I'd go back if something like this happened."

"Shut up, Dak. We didn't die. Be grateful. We've come too far."

Dakota was obviously and more than noticeably indignant, but he uttered nothing more.

"So what is it?" Said Kyle with a stern face. "You all want to return home—a god awful miserable place where no one likes us and everyone sucks?"

No one spoke.

"I'm still in." Brandon broke the silence. "We're fine now."

"'Leave it up to Jordan." Dak interjected. "This is all for him."

"We'll keep going." Jordan said, throwing his pack off. "And don't try to say you're doing this just for me. We all wanted to come."

"I lost the map." Said Brandon.

"Well that's great." Replied Erik.

"--It's fine." Kyle interrupted. "I still have a compass. It's more important; and from what I can tell, we're close to the border. We saved weeks."

"We need a fire. We're already in the first stages of hypothermia." Said Jordan, now calmer. "Maybe it was a stupid idea, maybe not, but we've made progress and know better now."

They couldn't disagree.

"I'll think more next time." Admitted Kyle. "We'll be more careful from now on. Now let's make a fire."

Chapter 7

Meeting Violet

It took about one to two days, but they boys finally let go of the river scenario and no longer blamed Kyle. The latter boy could tell they were getting closer, seeing as how easily they forgave their misgivings and forgot about them. The five of them had always been near at the hip, yet, despite arguing more in the wilderness, they held less against one another. They all secretly knew, or at least had a semblance of thought, that they had to unequivocally rely on each other. They were in the Devil's charted territory, without hope of finding anyone else to hold their shoulders, should they have distanced themselves.

The physical toil of the trip was becoming evermore pronounced as they continued. They still had nearly 2,000 miles left and enduring pain and getting tougher was essential. All of the boys had at least two blisters on their feet, and they'd awake to severe stiffness and sores. On every occasion, they felt ill of beginning another daily 20-30 miles, but they never gave in to apathy or antipathy. Their minds were fixed on a common goal; and that: *determination for a deep-seated grail*, will drive anyone to pursue any lengths–no matter the distance.

Despite all of that, they calculated (from memorizing the map) that they would reach the border in only two days, and, again, the subject of hitchhiking was brought up. There was certainly at least one major highway that ran across it. It took a gross amount of deliberation, but, against Kyle's wishes, they agreed upon doing it.

One could infer that hardship was the main cause, but moreso, it concerned a matter of time. They had sped up enormously, sure; but the aim to graduate was still in the back of most of their heads. That's not to factor in Winter–which was right at the doors–and they hoped to hike in the snow as little as possible.

Kyle felt no less than disdain at the idea, finding the whole point of the adventure to be null if they subsisted off the mercies of man, but he couldn't argue that it'd be better for Jordan, whom he secretly wanted to return home in one piece as quickly as possible. The poor kid appeared to wear down as the days went on–not terribly so, but noticeable, especially to someone like Kyle who was aware of his disease. As much as Kyle dreamt of being the leader, he'd often find himself staying in the back of the line with Jordan, who had difficulty catching up.

The morning before they were set to cross into Canada was the worst one yet. Just as they'd finally moved on from pointing fingers over the river debacle, discord broke out.

Kyle was the first to get up, start a fire, and went to nab a can of corn beef hash when he found two cans missing. His eyes grew red as he thought about the culprit. He demanded Brandon get up and explain himself.

The group was already losing patience with him. His pranks had become more frequent, and the teasing was overly-stressing them out. Two nights before, he'd taken ahold of Kyle's sleeping bag while he was away, placed some of his clothes and tools in it, and hung it up into a tree as a joke. The bag ended up tearing a little, and Kyle was forced to repair it with some duct tape, for which he was very, very not happy about.

Brandon emerged from his tent, still half-asleep and vexed, wondering what Kyle could possibly want.

"You did it again, didn't you? You jerk." Said Kyle, pointing to the bag of cans.

"Relax, Kyle. Today's the day, I swear. I'm going to go hunting. How am I supposed to catch food if I'm starving?"

By this time, the rest had overheard the arguing and rose equally mad. Erik, in particular.

"Why would you do that, Brandon!?" He shouted. "It's not a joke. We have to eat too."

"You promised us." Said Dak.

"It was just two measly cans. Look, I'll take my pellet gun right now and get us some birds."

He took his gun and went into the forest without hesitation. Meanwhile, the rest of the boys grundled and shared their irritation. After an hour of Brandon not being back, they began to pack up the tent and their belongings. They stood around waiting for him, even shouting his name at times—all for naught.

"I'm leaving." Said Dak.

"What are you talking about?" Replied Jordan. "We're going to wait for him. Maybe he will come back with something."

"And stay with him and let him starve us to death? He can catch up with us down the road. There's no wasting time today."

Dak began to walk into the woods down a small and thin game trail. Sheepishly, while looking back-and-forth, Erik and Kyle followed him. Jordan was stuck there, alone, not knowing what to do or which side to choose. He didn't have any food himself and couldn't risk being stranded without supplies alongside Brandon. Most of all, he couldn't be without Kyle. Slowly, continuously looking behind him and yelling for Brandon, he went down the trail.

The boys got about 500 feet away when Kyle, who was in the lead, stopped, and said they had to go back. Jordan agreed, while Dak stayed adamant with his position. Erik said nothing. It was decided that the group would stay there while Kyle went back for Brandon.

When he got back to the campsite, he found Brandon sitting on a log and crying. Beside him was a collection of dead birds and squirrels.

"I'm sorry, man." Was all Kyle could say.

"I thought you guys left me." He said.

"I wouldn't let them do that. You're just as much my friend as any of them. Sorry for getting so upset. It doesn't matter anymore."

Kyle helped Brandon get his things and they went to meet with the others down the way.

It was silent at first, between the group and Brandon, whose eyes were still teary. Dak couldn't help but feel bad and happy, especially considering that he got them food as he had promised. Erik felt guilty the most. Brandon and him were as close as Kyle was to Jordan. He should have never left him behind. They ended up hugging it out and the situation, like the river, was quickly forgotten about and forgave. In hindsight, Kyle thought it was a stupid thing to get so upset over.

It was that action that put the nail in the coffin of their bonding. Even Dak was closer to

Brandon. He'd always been, but they didn't bicker as much from then onward. Understanding that hurdles such as those would happen should have been plain before they even left. Their shared naivety was slowly dissolving, and, about that point, they truly recognized that each was equal and a member of their immediate family.

At last, about 10 grueling hours later, they made it into British Columbia and walked beside the dark, cold, rainy road, holding their thumbs out, and hoping someone could bring salvation from the dreary climate.

Luckily for them, this highway was, in fact, very popular, and it only took 11 cars passing their way until one stopped to lend a hand. Again, it was a Ford, and they hoped on the back. The driver was heading Northward of the province for business—perfect. They huddled down underneath a tarp the man had in the bed, and wrapped one of their blankets over themselves. It'd be a four hour drive. Indeed, any distance was better than none.

It was before sunrise when he had to set them free, about halfway up the province. Like the original hitch, the man stopped them in the woods; but this time, on a popular main trailhead that, for the most part, continued on way to either the Yukon or Northwest Territories as the crow flies. It was a difficult trail, but they expected nothing less. The terrain would get even more strenuous the deeper into the unknown they went.

Snow, lightly lit up by the moon, was falling heavily, and they debated whether to begin right away or wait for the sun to appear. By-and-by, they chose the former. And yet, it was a beautiful verdict. Almost immediately, they had hiked up to a good and high part of the hills which was lit to an extraordinary degree by the blue moonlight. The air was utterly bone-chilling, and they had to put on their winter clothes to the fullest; thankfully they prepared for it. Notwithstanding, their attire was not strong enough to keep them comfortably warm and they hoped to make outfits out of deer/elk skins and pelts.

They continued on the trail as they had done for another week, but the weather proved to be far harsher. Fires were more laborious to start (some days going without them), tents held less heat, darkness took over a greater part of the days, etc.; and yet, the prized food and water was more plentiful. Most days, they'd hunt at least 8 birds and small game creatures with their meager, weak gun. Brandon had even managed to kill some with his spears. They were accustomed to the cold, but had yet to dwell in snow and much lower temperatures. It wasn't even winter yet, and they had to straighten up a lot if they were going to survive Alaska.

Indeed, the trail was, in actuality, very popular, but less so at that time of year. They'd occasionally run into hardy, slightly crazy people, but they were hunters, more often than not. That was until they met Violet.

She came upon them one evening, and were slightly confused why a lithe, unassuming woman would be alone so deep into the woods.

She had caught up with them from behind and was going in the same direction, for what reason they thought to join her, even figuring she'd encourage them to move quicker.

She was 27 years old, and explained her life story, filling up the extended hours when they'd run out of things to talk about. Apparently, she was married for five years until her husband began to drink and become abusive. She divorced him months prior and, like the rest, felt she needed a break from civilization and their stressors. She'd never had time to herself, living so fast paced through college, straightaway into the workforce. The boys–especially Kyle–could positively sympathize and relate to her.

They'd continue with each other and camp every day, and it seemed as though Dak (who was 18 by that time) was taking a particular interest in her, despite the fairly wide age gap. He'd stay up with her past midnight, chatting variously about their common interests and what they hoped to do once back home. Oddly enough, she lived in Washington too, but a bit away from them in Seattle. He could absolutely see why she'd want to break free from there, and Kyle even overheard him inquire about visiting her.

Perhaps they could establish a link most because of their personalities. Like Dak, she was a very shy and reserved individual while in school, and was often scared of trying new things. She, just as he, took a big leap to trek such a long way. She never regretted it, and Dak was beginning not only to accept where he was, but embrace it fully finally. She persuaded him that their adventure was more than just hiking, and there came to the surface a peculiar, almost religious sixth sense that was awakened in the undisturbed, secluded land. In Dak's eyes (though he wouldn't say it), she was not only a love interest, but an inspiration.

They got to know her better than most over the following two weeks. She had no destination in mind and wanted to journey along with them as long as she could, it seemed. She was, indeed, one of the kindest people they'd ever met. She spoke poetically and talked about nature a lot, just like Kyle, who adored her mindset and heart. She also appeared to be somewhat of a tomboy; not outwardly, but psychologically. She'd practice pellet gun shooting with Dak and managed to kill quite a bit of fowl and creepers herself.

Kyle went out to scoop up some water from a nearly-frozen pond one morning and saw Dak and her sitting near it, kissing. It honestly made him happy. Dak had been suffering a difficult time since they'd left, and it was nice to see him find something (or someone) he loved. Sure, it was weird that she was nine years his senior, but if it made him complain less and show more appreciation for his surroundings, then the group as a whole was most supportive of it.

Dak related to Jordan eventually that he considered going along with her back to the states. Jordan, although empathetic towards his feelings, quickly shut down the idea. He wasn't upset by any means, but instilled just how close of a team they were, and they honestly needed Dak. It was the first instance when he felt profoundly appreciated, and his consideration was instantly renounced. He knew just how stupid it was also, and he was being rendered unsighted by his passions.

Later that same night, the two slept beneath the glowing, snowy sky, freezing in their reinforced sleeping bags. When Dak awoke in the morning, he found a note in his bag with Violet nowhere in sight. There were little words on it–saying only that she had to leave with an address below it. He was despondent, even feeling a sliver of forlornness, but he likely understood, and, at any rate, she wanted him to visit. He was fairly content.

Chapter 8

The Foresters

The nameless mountain was high and intimidating as they approached it. No longer would they have the easy way out of journeying in-between the hills and ridges; this trail was long, onerous, and unforgiving. It wasn't, however, new. They had grown extremely accustomed to pushing their bodies to the limit, with calves of iron, backs of timber, and feet of stone, but that mountain in particular was unusually high and menacing. Much of its sides were blanketed in cliffs or steep rock faces. Many Big Horns found sanctuary on it. No matter, they thought, they'd prevail, regardless of how long it took for them to conquer it.

Indeed, the start wasn't horrendous. Mid-way down the mountain were all trees and switchbacks. Still very steep and with an endless inclination, they frequently had to pause to rest, but there wasn't a step they couldn't overcome. It changed the higher they got.

There came a noticeable—and fairly ominous, frankly—point near the peak, where the trail ran just along the side of a cliff. They knew if they could get through the huddle, it'd be a smooth ride down directly afterwards when they again entered the treeline.

They stood before the narrow trail, looking forward at its relation to the height. If they fell, death's grip was a guarantee. As much as they'd grown since leaving, they were all extremely scared of moving forward, save Kyle, who decided to take the reins.

He proposed that they went one at a time with the stroller being tethered to the rest of them. Even if tall Brandon fell, the remaining four of them shouldn't have had any trouble hoisting him back up.

They looked at him in silence, with somewhat large eyes. The path, from side-to-side, was only about two feet and their fears—which were justified—were getting the best of him. Again trying to be leader of the pack, Kyle decided to go first.

The other boys held the rope as tight as they could; so much so that Kyle had to keep yelling at them to let up on it and give him some slack to go forward. He moved slowly and methodically, attempting not to look at the abyss below, but it proved almost impossible, having to stare at the trail so thin. At one point, vertigo was beginning to take hold of him and he was forced to stop, close his eyes, and lean against the wall. He was likely the bravest out of them, and it worried him that it'd all be for naught and he'd have to pass through the ledge again when the others didn't show up.

One step at a time, he made it through to the other side. The light sweat on his face immediately began to freeze once he cooled down and released a breath of relief.

"Okay, you guys ready!?" He shouted from the other side.

All the boys looked at one another, trying to act gentleman-like and let someone go before them. Finally Jordan stepped forward and tied the rope to his waist. The rest cheered him on with words of encouragement. Being so light and small, he was the most nimble, ideal kid to go.

Like a champion, he let no foreign fear overshadow his mind, and walked swiftly across it–hardly showing an ounce of dismay. The two (but Jordan, especially) making it safely encouraged Dak, Erik, and Brandon. Brandon's turn was next. At this point, Erik and Dak held a rope, while Jordan and Kyle did likewise; both harnessed to big Brandon.

Out of nowhere, to everyone's surprise, he quickly ran across it without any concern or hesitancy. The boys wanted to get mad and call him stupid, but they were too overpowered with ease and disbelief that he was okay.

What was really perplexing–but maybe not, at that point–was Dak wanting to go before Erik. They worried most for him and should have forced him to try it sooner. If he was the last one, got cold feet, and was utterly adamant about refusing, they'd all have to go back.

"Run like me, Dak!" Shouted Brandon. "It's faster and you don't get dizzy."

"No, Brandon." Said Jordan. "It's too dangerous."

"It's up to you, Dak. Whatever you feel comfortable with." Exclaimed Kyle.

Dak paused for a moment, tightening the knot around his waist as hard as he possibly could. He took a deep breath and, in an instant, he bolted across and fell into the group, who swiftly congratulated him.

"Alright, Erik! Last one, man. You got this!" Said Brandon.

"I'm going to run, too!" He said, with his words getting caught by the strong breeze.

At once, Erik sprinted until, about five feet in, his foot slipped on the edge. He was thrown off–slicing his leg along the way. He hung for dear life, shouting loudly, not even acknowledging the blood running down his thigh.

"Pull me up! Pull, god dammit!"

He squeezed his eyes shut, refusing to look down.

"It's okay! We got you man!" Yelled Kyle, amidst all the commotion and shouting.

The four of them lifted their chests and, in a solid line, used all their might to pull him up. Once he got to his feet, he hugged them as though his life depended on it.

"Oh crap, Erik, your leg." Said Kyle.

Erik looked down in horror, but mostly with shock. The amount of adrenaline numbed any semblance of pain he'd normally have.

Kyle threw off his pack and pulled a t-shirt out of it. Without thought, he tore it apart and wrapped it tightly around the wound–trying his best to suffocate the gash. It was bad, but not the worst. It could have healed fine without stitches, though he could certainly have used some.

"We won't do anything like this again." Kyle said calmly. "We'll go around a mountain if we have to."

They rested there for a good hour, letting their minds mollify and giving Erik a moment of relaxation. They were forced to make a crutch after he had a difficult time standing for long periods of time. It'd slow them down, but there were no alternatives. Regardless, no speed is worse than death.

It was a little past noon, and they were set to at least get to ground-level before the end of the day; more than doable. The descent was pleasant (albeit hard on the joints), but proved difficult for Erik, who had to be supported by Brandon much of the way. Kyle (although, the others too), was quite proud of him for taking his situation so well. His physical vigor through the pain was applaudable, but his mental fervor for continuing on, moreso.

When they eventually did get below, they were prepared to stop and set camp when they heard a bunch of noise a little ways in the distance. Assuming it may be a chance to get some sort of supplies or food—or even simply out of curiosity—they decided to keep going and check it out.

They were unexpectedly met with a road and large groups of campsites. At this time, they still had little clue where they were in the grand scheme of things, only they were going in the right direction by way of the compass.

They considered going over to one of them, but weren't sure if it was a good idea. All of the only three spots were taken, which was unfortunate, seeing as how nice and neat the place was. There was a moderately large group of folks with a gigantic bonfire in the center of them, and they boys couldn't help but go over and attempt to join them briefly. Snow was beginning to fall heavily and the darkness was setting in. It would have been a terrible chore to keep moving, find somewhere, and build a fire in the snowy night.

Oddly (or maybe not), the people were exceedingly nice and welcoming. Once catching eye of Erik and his crutch, they immediately took them in and let them stay the night.

There were six of them: four men and two women—all foresters. They planned to spend a month in the woods and progressively clear logs off of the trails and do repairs where needed. Kyle took a liking to that idea. One could tell just how acquainted they were to the outdoors. The men were scruffy, bigly built with thick, long beards. All of them held revolvers on their sides and had at least a dozen axes lying about. Most attractive of all: their large caches of very good, tasty food.

The foresters had no spare tents, but they did have a plethora of tarps and wool blankets they let the boys use. It can be conjectured that, like the boys, they had sort of a campsite cabin fever of isolation or loneliness, for which reason they were such an exemplary agreeable and neighborly folk to them. Indeed, isolation was something to admire, and Kyle's ultimate dream, but it's human nature to be around at least one person, lest the recluse goes mad. The foresters had already been there for three weeks, and one can imagine they were tiring of one another. That would never happen to the runaways.

It wasn't very long until the boy's somewhat gave a falsified account of their travels. They had no doubt that the foresters could ever do something if they did end up saying their motives, but Kyle simply explained that they were college graduates (obviously not by appearance, save Brandon) and journeying through the Canadian wilderness was the graduation celebration. It was an easy sell. They were truthful, however, with relaying the things and hardships they'd endured. The forest servicers were impressed how they had survived so long with only a spring tent, one pair of winter clothes, and subsisting off small critters like birds and foxes.

It was because of that respect that they offered their food to them. Still dried food, for the most part, everything they had were delicacies. Being nearly winter, they had a good amount of frozen food, as well. Things like warm pasta, heated up meatloaf, chips, cookies, beef, and bacon–items of immense value, pleasure, and sensational dissipation. Indeed, they were all worth their weight in gold.

It was about 9:00 and, after filling their gullets, they were offered alcohol and cigarettes; the former being under the presumption they were of age. Naturally, the feelings of drunkenness and nicotine buzzes completely overshadowed their newfound extreme appreciation of food.

Jordan, the poor kid, couldn't drink. He was already weak and in a constant state of pain. Kyle began to worry evermore for him as the days went on, and felt helpless. He was rapidly losing weight in the last week, and Kyle, for the most part, had to force him to eat at every meal behind the pack's back. Jordan's best friend was starting to fill up his mind and thoughts more and more. Kyle initially thought the trip would be healthy and therapeutic for him. He was seriously considering his ignorance, and prayed often that his illness slowed, at least until they got back. He could shake the idea—as much as he tried—that he made the wrong decision of letting him come, even though it was Jordan's scheme. Guilt gradually crept up and depressed his mind. There was a very, very faint constant thought that they should turn back for him. He'd eventually bring it up to him.

Kyle didn't know how much longer they could keep it a secret from the rest of the boys. His eyes kept getting yellower and Jordan usually staggered behind when hiking–by far having to take more breaks than the rest, which Kyle defended, using the excuse of his small, lithe stature. He wished his friend could rest every other day: if only it was an option. They had, however, been justifying Jordan's symptoms with simply having the flu. They all believed it, but would surely end up being skeptical of the fact that no one else got it, and Jordan had suffered from it for "two weeks" at that point.

While Erik's wounds were being tended to by one of the women (Edith), Kyle sat beside one of the burly men named, Arthur. He was a man who'd appeared to truly live. Just about every second of the day, he'd gently sip whiskey and smoke out of an old, black pipe. Kyle related his desire and life goal of living off the land and, incidentally, Arthur had done just that.

Before becoming a forester (out of love for the woods), he was a cattle rancher and, after making enough money, trekked on horseback all across the states, from British Columbia all the way to the Nevada desert. He was a fervent and fairly famous hunter in America, but chose to migrate to a place even freer of people—just like Kyle.

He would go on and on—forever, if Kyle let him—of his wild and spectacular tales roughing it out like the old westerners and pioneers. It was quite inspiring to Kyle and made the kid a little envious. He made him deeply contemplate over becoming a forester himself, or anyone who worked for the wild period. Kyle felt stupid for the thought never having occurred or crossed his mind.

It was quite nice. Kyle could connect and share his perspective with him perhaps more than anyone. His friends had a very deep passion for the outdoors, Jordan in particular, but not as much as him. At Kyle's choosing, he'd spend the rest of his years secluded in an Alaskan cabin, subsisting off the bounties of nature, and living a peaceful life of meditating silence and stillness.

Arthur presented the option to him of letting them stay for a few days if they wanted. Kyle wasn't sure. For one, he didn't know if the man was only saying that out of his stupor, but he still wasn't attracted to the idea of staying put at all. Then again, they'd made it a long way, and it was only the 18th of December. God only knew how long it'd take them to get back to Washington.

With the thought of Washington came the thought of home. He pondered what his parents were doing and how they felt. Ignorantly, he figured they were hardly concerned–probably eating dinner while sipping wine in quietness like usual. He did, however, know that they weren't living their lives precisely the same way. He only wished they could understand how pleased he was after his woodsy rebirth and baptism.

Arthur, after getting thoroughly intoxicated, went to bed about 11:00, and Kyle, being a lightweight, slowly dazed off to sleep against the log.

He awoke in the morning, finding himself covered with two blankets, sitting right on a couple inches of snow. He thought it sort of humorous that they kept him warm, yet let him spend all night on the freezing ground.

Everyone was up and the adults were already in the full swing of cooking breakfast, which he was naturally disposed to. He went up to them, taking five pieces of bacon from the food tray, scarfing them down in an instant.

Arthur, still half-drunk, stood around them sipping a beer, informing the rest that Kyle and his friends would be staying the coming days with them. The last thing the kid wanted to do was impose and take all of their foodstuffs, and he still wasn't sure if it was just the alcohol talking, but the other foresters seemed more than happy with it. Even by 8:30 AM, there was nearly a blizzard forming, and the last thing the boys wanted to do was hike and get lost and swept up into the lottery of foggy directions.

Chapter 9

Northbound

The following two and a half days were exceedingly agreeable. Arthur–perhaps out of his drunkenness–was always the most outgoing and would continuously teach the boys new skills, appearing to take a particular fondness towards Kyle; perhaps he knew the boy looked up to him, despite only meeting days ago.

After showing Kyle and Jordan how to throw hatchets properly one morning, Brandon and Erik essentially begged him to go hunting and allow them to use his rifle. He was more than happy to oblige. Kyle longed to join them, and surely knew that they'd have to start hunting big game eventually, but was still saddened by the idea. For being such an wildly ambitious, adventurous, rugged boy, a good amount of his mind was sensitive and his heart (at least when it came to the natural world) would often take priority over his head. Still, he was not against the idea, knowing well the idiom: *survival of the fittest*, but if he had choice of any kind, he'd always decline to kill anything.

As Kyle sharpened his knives beside the fire colliding with snowflakes, he saw Brandon and Dak emerging through the treeline, yelling cheerfully, and holding a large deer on a log.

"We got one!" Exclaimed Erik.

"Damn heavy." Brandon said, as he set it in the snow.

"Alright, even though it's cold, we have to clean it very fast. Who wants to do it?" Arthur looked around.

The boys all glanced at one another, slightly grossed out by the thought of it.

"Why don't you, Brandon? You caught it; you deserve to." Said Jordan.

"Yeah, and you're used to gutting birds." Replied Dak.

"Alright, you pansies."

Brandon took his buck knife and had his way into the innards, attempting to not gag most of the way. After a couple of minutes, he was finished and the rest of the boys graduated him.

They threw the unappealing guts into the fire, while keeping the heart and liver. Arthur demonstrated how to skin it, filet the meat, and smoke it quickly. They were all almost mesmerized at the sight of it, trying to retain the information while holding back their adrenaline-fueled excitement. Their latent acestoral, primitive essences had been awakened.

They ate well that night. Cookies and bacon were good, but to devour and savor steak one caught themselves tasted far better, and more than it normally would have at a restaurant.

As they ripped meat off of bones, they informed the foresters that they'd have to leave in the morning. Both groups were a little sorrowful at the mention of it, but the boys couldn't stay there forever. Genuinely, the main reason Kyle chose to stay was for Jordan. The kid needed a break, rest, and good food. Even so, it wasn't like they were on vacation and could drive home any day. They had a long way yet to travel.

The foresters were kind enough to let the group take as much of the deer meat as they could. All in all, they had enough to last them about 11 days—more if they rationed.

Though Kyle felt they were foisting themselves onto them, the truth was, that the foresters had little to do at the time being, and Kyle provided entertainment. The mountain folk needed something to curb their despondently dull waiting.

About 6:00 AM, they headed out, forcing their heavy packs back onto their still-sore shoulders.

The freezing fog was thick and suffocating, but it dissolved into a thin mist only an hour later. The weather was not infinitely ideal, but, with only three inches or snow and a mostly-clear line of vision, it was more than perfect to the group.

Luckily and incidentally, the main road went northbound for a distance, so they had the ease of walking along it.

After about three hours on the snowy dirt road, a shadow suddenly appeared in front of them through the mist. Curious, and thinking it was only a coyote or deer, they continued until, out of nowhere, its true form was revealed.

10 feet away was a small, tan cougar, facing them with a menacing disposition. Immediately, the boys stopped in their tracks. Erik broke the silence by gently exclaiming a mimicking hiss.

"Shut up, Erik." Kyle whispered.

Kyle told them to raise their arms and back up slowly. The cat occasionally followed them and showed its teeth, but, after 15 minutes, finally decided to run away into the trees. It likely wanted to do no harm and was more scared of them, but it was indeed, a highlight of the week.

Seven miles later, while snacking on their deer jerky, they saw a railroad track cutting across the road. There just so happened to be a train seen not far down it, so they chose to examine it. In the far distance, a conductor was walking around in the front with an oil lamp. They had to stay hidden. Disappearing behind carts and running to the next ones, they finally found one open.

"Where 'you headed?" Said a voice coming from inside the darkness, making Jordan jump with surprise.

"Anywhere North." Said Jordan.

"You're in luck, kid. We're heading up to the Yukon."

"Can we join you?"

The mysterious man peered through the shadows and gave Jordan his hand to help him up. The boys quickly did the same.

"We're not going to get caught, are we?" Asked Dak.

"Nah." Another man said, swatting his arm. "There's no bulls here; too remote."

The two older men were fairly scruffy looking, and it was apparent they were homeless. They introduced themselves as Will and Arlo.

Will brought out a smoke and offered some to them. Their eyes lit up in an instant, having run out of cigarettes long ago and suffered their lungs being sober. Save Jordan, they all took deep puffs, and relaxed their backs against the wall, experiencing a buzz they hadn't felt in what must have been forever.

In a sense, they were a little happy they'd lost their addictions–at least until they got back. To be dependent on man's drugs is to be dependent on man himself. They wanted only to be at the mercy of themselves and the wild.

Will seemed to be a man with his head tightly on his shoulders, but Alro was a bit of an inane individual, falling in and out of sleep every five minutes.

"What's his story?" Jordan asked, pointing at the passed out man.

"Some guy I'd met down South. He was already on this train when I joined him. 'Never spoke much about himself; only that he was homeless. Probably is on here just for shelter."

"And you?"

The man's countenance suddenly turned to a depressing image.

"My little boy passed away two months ago. I killed both my wife and me, and she couldn't bear it, so she and I separated. She took the house—and I don't hold it against her—but I had nowhere else to go. So I quit my job and decided to escape the town. I don't want to be reminded of that life."

"You don't know where you're going?"

"Nope, and that's the way I like it. When I find the right place, I'll hop off for good."

Suddenly, Arlo sprang to life in a happy state, as though he got surprised, and went right back to sleep thereafter, before anyone could respond.

The boys told him their story–but this time with sincerity and truthfulness. The man wouldn't judge nor have the wherewithal to mention it to outsiders. Oddly, he didn't greatly sympathize with them. He found them dumb for forsaking good, loving lives, and hurting those who cared for them. Kyle understood where he was coming from, despite disagreeing. To Kyle, he *had* to do what he was doing. He didn't appreciate his old life as much as the man did. In a way, he was in the same position: both wanted to find a better home; the originator of the concept was just different.

Will picked up a guitar beside him and started plucking some notes as he listened to Kyle, who felt that he wasn't being understood.

"Home is where you make it–you're right about that, kid; but sometimes being with loved ones, in safety and aegis, is where your true home lies."

Kyle sat silently, slightly annoyed that he didn't comprehend his plight. Will had his reasons–which were justified, but so did he, Kyle thought. The kid thought that them abandoning their lives was a necessity, and not so much a split decision. That train, about to speed onward to an unknown place, was a better home than with his parents.

"You're pretty good at that." Sad Dak, pointing to his guitar.

"Any of you ever played?"

"I did in middle school, but never since. It broke only after a couple months of getting it." Dak replied.

"That's a shame."

Will handed them each another cigarette, and as they rested, he began playing his own version of Big Rock Candy Mountain. The train then began to move.

Kyle went to sit and dangle his legs off the side of the cart, and watched the evening sun behind the falling snow. He must have stared out into the scenery for at least an hour, when he turned to find everyone asleep. He grabbed his notebook and started to scribble down some phrases he could potentially form into poetry. He would do so for a few more hours until night fell.

About that time, he'd manifested a full collection of sonnets and lyrics, which he hoped to look back on and read in the future. He aspired to eventually publish it and allow others to get a taste of their escapades once back.

The sun of the morning shone on his face, forcing his eyes to softly open. He saw Dak reading a note beside the guitar with Will and Arlo missing. It read: *"Dear kid, the top string of the guitar is broken. I used to play it with my son and could never throw it away with the memories. I guess it's time I let it go and end the bad ones on a good note. Play it for him, will ya?"*

Chapter 10

By The Sea

The unknown, unnamed train was an unexpectedly serene and gratifying home for a brief stint. They remained on it for well over two days, likely being dehydrated if not for the constant pouring of snow.

They'd pass into Winter about three and a half weeks before and, in spite of the cold, their combined body heat warmed the small, humble cart. It was all quite agreeable. They hadn't a clue where they were headed; only eventually finding the direction Westward with the divine, cherished compass.

At one point, their ride made a slow turn and relocated East. It was then that they felt their excursion had provided all it could, and decided to hop off and continue on foot. They had certainly made a good number of miles, and prayed they were now in the Yukon.

The locomotive's turn-around occurred not long after it began one day. They knew they'd have to jump, or else risk losing hundreds of miles.

They stood at the edge, trying to gauge how fast it was moving but it didn't matter–it was going too fast for comfort. For whatever reason, Jordan had once learned that parachute jumpers had a special way to land. They land on their feet with little pressure, then roll on the side of their legs. The same principle should have applied, he thought.

They waited until they approached a large pile(s) of snow they could float in. A couple minutes passed when they saw a good spot quickly coming up in the distance.

"Alright; on three." Said Kyle. "One, two, three–"

At high speed, they leapt into a heap of white cotton, instantly plummeting to the bottom. It took a second for them to resurface from the deep snow but, when they did, they couldn't help but laugh. Thankfully, and surprisingly, none of them got hurt.

In the face of occasional large lumps, the overall snow levels weren't too bad, but they knew they'd have to get/make snowshoes in the not too distant future. Walking in even two inches of snow takes more energy than it would otherwise, and their speed would diminish enormously if they had to wade through four feet.

Again, they were back on foot. Assuming they were higher North (than they really were), they chose to hike straight towards the West, hoping Alaska was not an eternity away.

The setting, then, was one of the most revered for Kyle. The thick, endless pine trees and firs being covered and weighed down by snow, with infinite small bright white mounds glowing from the clear day's sun, was exemplary and beautiful. In such a climate, all animals and fowl of every kind are exposed. The fox cannot blend in with the snowy ground and likewise, the hawk or eagle with the trees.

In some ways, it was easier to trek through snow and in others, more difficult. Better, because you can walk above all of the small branches, sticks, and rocks and not trip as one would commonly do; harder, because such things are cloaked and, if you do get caught, you'll keep falling. The directions were, indeed, far easier, being able to fully see where one can walk without the overwhelming distraction of countless brambles and thickets.

They continued on for a few hours, often having to either add or strip layers off their bodies due to the heat versus cold of hiking.

They ended up facing a moderately-sized stream. It cut them straight off from continuing West and they'd no idea when they could get around it. They made the decision to cross it, but with reluctance.

This time, getting swept away or drowning wasn't a concern in the slightest, but if they fell, they'd be soaked. Hypothermia would kick in fast.

They all took a hold of long hiking sticks and, in a line, gently and methodically went across stones step-by-step.

Fortunately, they were luckier than they were before and came out the other side unscathed.

"Do you smell that?" Asked Erik. "It's salty, like the ocean."

"We can't possibly be that West, can we?" Asked Brandon.

"Let's keep going. Maybe best to see if we are." Kyle replied.

The smell of the sea only got stronger the further they walked. Finally, two hours later, they found themselves on a large, desolate, and freezing beach.

What they didn't know was that they *were* in Alaska–albeit a small strip of it. They stood directly Westward of Juneau and Whitehorse, and midway between the state and province's cities. They had to have only been six miles from the Yukon-Alaska border.

Yet, they hadn't that idea and couldn't figure out which one they were in. In their minds, if it *was* the Yukon, it was only a sliver of it, and it was more than likely Alaska. Naturally, this was a very exciting thought.

They set up camp far up near the bank. In spite of less snow, the beach was far, far colder than the mainland, but in a sense, that's how they—or at least Kyle—liked it.

While Kyle attempted to conjure up a fire, the others got it in their heads to make primitive fishing poles or crab traps. For an odd reason, difficult to put a finger on, a burst of exhilaration and elation grew in them. Perhaps it was due to being in Alaska finally, or being able to get good food; likely a combination of both.

Between the wind, cold, and wetness, the fire was painstaking. Kyle had worked on lighting it for at least an hour, but was running out of his cumulative matches and about to give up. Finally, he chose to rip out and use some of his notepad paper. It meant less poems, but heat and light were more important. At last, a smolder turned into a bonfire.

As Jordan and Kyle sat beside it, Brandon came over with his pathetic and dumb-looking pole, holding up a caught mackerel-sized fish and looking proud.

"It won't feed us much, but it's something."

"It's one bite worth of food, Brandon." Jordan joked.

"Guys! Come look at this!" Came a loud, yet faint, yell from Dak far down the beach.

As they got over to him, they found an endless sea of muscles, clams, and cockles scattered about. On top of that, innumerable crabs scurried around, getting their fill on dead shellfish.

In an instant, the boys filled up their arms with as many as they could possibly muster, running back and forth between the buffet and fire. Meanwhile, Jordan, Dak, and Erik began making spears to kill the crabs.

They ate extraordinarily well that evening. They buried the shellfish and crabs in hot ash and feasted off them until their stomachs had their fill. It hadn't been since their meeting with the foresters that they didn't feel at least a little hungry.

As they sat talking and joking, the beach below them began to glow blue. Never having seen or heard of such a thing, they went down to find a landscape of small, glowing jellyfish. Brandon scooped some up, for which he got scolded.

"They could be toxic, you dunce!" Said Erik.

"They're not stinging me. Relax." He dropped them. "Hey, we should go back. I got a surprise for Jordan."

"A surprise?" Jordan asked, with a confused expression.

Once they returned, Brandon pulled out a box of squished twinkies and a bottle of vodka.

"Did you steal those?" Asked Kyle.

"Just the alcohol, but they wouldn't have cared. Arthur let us drink as much as we wanted."

Kyle was, naturally, a little annoyed at him, but brushed it off.

"Here, Jordan." Said Brandon. "You get the first drink and twinkies."

"For what, Brandon?"

"Your birthday."

"My birthday was months ago."

"Come on, Jordan. You know you nor your asshole dad didn't do anything for it. This trip's for you, and we can at least thank you for getting it together."

It obviously made Jordan feel good, and he appreciated someone like Brandon being so altruistic.

"I don't feel like drinking, but I'll take some twinkies. You guys go for the vodka."

Brandon was confused why he'd said that, but didn't give much thought into it.

Though not knowing about the cancer, the rest of them always had a sense of grief towards the kid. He lived a hard life and never seemed to be able to catch a break (until then). It made Kyle especially happy, knowing just how much worse

Jordan's life was at present than any of the others knew.

That's not factoring in his physicality. Being the smallest with the least muscle, the trip must have been hardest on his body. Yet, surely, the others must have begun to question his appearance. Whereas the whole lot of them became stronger and bulkier due to it, Jordan only withered more and more. It was, indeed, miraculous that he managed to keep up with them. To Kyle's relief, Jordan had no trouble downing the twinkies every time he handed him one.

They, and even Kyle, essentially spent the remainder of the night getting drunk and dancing around the campfire that only got larger and larger. Towards the end of it—which pretty much marked the end of being awake—Erik was the most drunk and instilled in Brandon that he had something important to say. Everyone was curious and anticipated either a joke or deep thought, but he ended up keeling over and passing out before he could get to it, which the others found funny.

It was about three in the morning when Kyle was jolted up by the sound of great thunder. Out of their stupor, they hadn't even realized a large storm had been brewing over the last hours, with mass wind and rain rattling the meager tent. It seemed that, as every minute passed, the wind got only evermore powerful, until the point when one of the poles snapped.

At that point, the whole group was awake, and fearful.

Kyle believed he could hear the ocean waves too well and, once opening the zipper, saw the tide ready to violently kiss the tent. They shouldn't have stayed on the sand. He immediately screamed for everyone to get their things and abandon the tent, lest they remained and be swept out to sea.

In a hurry and filled with adrenaline, they harshly dragged their belongings out while stepping into the lowly waves. Narrowly, they had escaped before watching the broken, tattered tent float out into the black, stormy ocean.

They had no time to realize their wetness; instead desperately searching for shelter as the gale, lightning, and downpour ensued. With nowhere to go, they made a run for the tightnit trees and huddled against one another. Thankfully, they had a poncho with them. They cut it up and held it over them.

They examined their blankets but found them all either drenched or mostly wet. They were already in the first stages of hypothermia and grew exceedingly scared. Building a fire would prove impossible. The only choice they had was to wait it out and combine their body heat as best they could.

Finally, at 6:00 PM, the storm subsided and the venerable, holy sun began to shine. There was no more sleep after waking to the terror and they continued to mightily shiver. The sun gave warmth, but they weren't in the tropics. It was the longest, worst, and most frightening night of their lives.

Again, at daybreak, the idea of lighting a fire came up, but they unanimously knew the unlikeliness of it.

Their plans, for the moment, were utterly destroyed. Instead of walking up the coast, they'd have to go to either Whitehorse or Juneau—the former being the best option. They couldn't hope to survive another night without a shelter or dry blankets. They needed warmth.

They forced themselves to walk cold and wet and brought out the hallowed compass, praying their theoretical speculation of a direction would take them to civilization; hopefully only temporarily.

Chapter 11

The Safety of Whitehorse

The day was grueling, toilsome, miserable. Their bodies had heated up, walking through heavy snow, but at any break would their wet clothes quickly absorb all coldness in the air. Their hair never dried an iota, and even with their beanies on, their ears had long since had feelings in them. They had to keep moving, and likely their only chance at mere surviving would be to make it into the city.

Kyle latched onto the compass as though his life depended on it–which may have been true. He was clueless if their wayward direction was even close to being correct but, seeing as how big Whitehorse was, he was confident there'd at least be many roads leading into it that they'd come across.

Indeed, they walked all the way into the next night, not bothering attempting to camp nor rest. It was at night when the fear really set in. Not only couldn't they see hardly six feet in front of them with their weak flashlights (that they'd been trying to conserve and not use), but the temperature had fallen at least another 30 degrees.

They threw their woolen blankets over themselves, as well as other insulated (yet soaked) clothes, which, ironically, did provide relief. As long as they kept moving.

The others would not say it, but Kyle knew they were scared: more so than they'd ever been before. Walking on severely numbed feet for nearly 17 hours in the pitch black forest, unsure of where they were going, and paranoid they'd never make it and suffer from acute hypothermia were the only things on their minds.

He knew them better than their own selves at times, and understood their fright. He too, felt it, but also sensing that he was the leader of the pack and mentally strongest one, he couldn't show weakness nor distress.

Kyle mollified them the best he could—pretending to be overly-confident in where they were heading, that they could put effort into making a fire in the morning, and their dire endurance would not last much longer. Any dried clothes he had, he gave and wrapped around Jordan, who was suffering the most. For emergencies, Kyle had brought a single body warmer that he was extremely reluctant to use. Finally, it came in handy, and he attached it to Jordan's back—supposedly helping immensely.

Jordan, as usual (though more than ever), would have to take frequent breaks. It didn't make the others happy, but Kyle, who was the leader in the line, always forced them to and came to Jordan's side.

Light finally dawned one hour, and they felt a great sense of relief. They had survived the unforgiving, desolate, and menacing night.

They decided they had to make a fire, if they could. The cold was unbearable and how much longer they'd have was not certain. The matches were safe and untouched by sea water; but, at any rate, they had magnesium and steel for back up. Kindling anything with the latter would take a godsend in that climate.

The boys were more than relieved to stop. Second to survival, their weary minds were only filled with thoughts of sleeping.

The morning was foggy. Kyle went around a small hill to find dry wood and moss, being careful not to get lost in the frosty haze. As he arose from bending down, he noticed a female elk about 15 feet in front of him. Beside her were three babies looking onward at him, curious but not necessarily scared.

It was very beautiful, he thought. They showed no hint of agitation or anxiety. He considered if they were his familiar spirits, giving him a good sign that they'd be alright.

Jordan yelled from around the other side, asking how close to being done Kyle was. The elk simply turned their heads towards the sound, and gently trodden away.

Kyle returned with small, hopefully dry sticks and witch's hair.

He removed snow from the ground and laid the materials in a teepee pile, tearing a good deal of paper out of his notebook–even a poem. He knew he had to give it his all. The group stood around him, staring at his hands and matches as though he was their lord, and they, sinners begging for mercy. He couldn't let them down.

It was the first match. Nothing. It stayed lit for no more than two seconds.

Kyle took a deep breath, then held it as he stroked another against the damp box.

This time, he lit the paper. It was promising, as the paper flamed up about seven inches. Then it went out.

"Dammit!" Kyle exclaimed.

There were only four useful matches left at this point; if they were exhausted, there'd be no chance of heat at that point.

At last, on the third strike, Kyle shoved the lit wooden stick inside the driest moss and held his breath as hard as he could. Suddenly, sparks began to ignite and, as softly as humanly possible, he blew into it ever so slightly.

Slowly but surely, the blessed fire began to spread and they had a meek, fiery stick. Carefully did they seldomly add more until a solid fire had been made.

The joy they felt at such a small, miniscule achievement was indescribable. Immediately were they up against it in a circle, huddling in as close as they could without burning themselves. After awhile, they had warmed up their faces, feet, and palms considerably, but they found it infeasible to add larger sticks or logs. They were too wet, too frozen. It was only a short stint that it stayed lit. After six beautiful minutes, the last minute flame had diminished.

Naturally, they were vexed and furious, instantly resuming to suffer the freezed wind. At any rate, however, they'd still have to journey to the city. They were without a tent and had saturated sleeping bags; they could not go on at their current state.

So it was that they continued their pace, praying to whatever god they could think of that they'd reach something–anything.

After two further hours had passed, by the divine grace of nature, they came upon a highway. At once, did they run to it and attempt to flag down cars. To their surprise, one soon stopped yet again: another pick-up fortuitously heading to Whitehorse.

Oblivious to just how far they walked, they were only a 15 minute drive from it. Again, did they cram themselves in the bed, colder than ever as the incessant wind smacked and slapped their numbed, redden cheeks; but they couldn't have been more pleased.

The thought arose in Kyle's mind how, despite never having had faith in man, he was at their mercy then, and that man was essentially saving his life. Perhaps they weren't all bad, he thought.

They eventually got into the city shortly there afterwards. It was a strange, now foreign feeling to them as they watched the bustling, busy people wandering about and the cars driving every which way. True, they'd been gone only a couple months, but that was enough time to alter their states of mind. Their primitive instincts and emotions had already come well to the surface, and what was once natural and accepted–that is, what people call "cities"--was then *foreign*–the preeminent word that best defined their adventure.

The first thing on their minds was to find some sort of shelter. It was loitering, but they simply walked into a store and pretended to be shopping. Finally, they found a reprieve and they could feel their appendages again. After a quarter of an hour, Kyle informed them that he was going to take Jordan to the hospital.

It can't be overstated how bad Jordan looked at that time. Once 140 pounds, he had shed nearly 25 off. His eyes were yellower than ever, he was having trouble standing, and the pain in his abdomen was becoming unbearable. Still, the others, completely ignorant that it was something more serious, thought he only had the flu–quite a foolish thought, knowing he'd been "sick" for the last month at least and the symptoms were not that of the common virus.

They accepted the idea and would meet them at the hospital at a later point, wanting to appreciate and relish the warmth as much as they could.

When the two boys got there, they related to the staff that they were homeless (which was an easy sell by their appearance), and that Jordan (telling them his name was "James") had cancer. Fairly altruistically, they accepted him right away, despite lacking insurance. They wouldn't do anything serious for free, but they were happy to examine the tumor.

The news was not good. It had progressed to a little over stage two and spread to his liver.

Kyle couldn't help but tear up when they said he needed treatment immediately or else...

The doctor provided him with a good amount of hydrocodone pills, lamenting the fact that "James" didn't have insurance.

At the very least, it made the two boys happy that he'd find relief from the pain for awhile.

The two left the hospital in a depressed state. Jordan remained silent until the other boys met with them. By this time, they had no choice. They'd have to admit what was affecting the kid, fearful of their reaction.

Kyle was the one to break the news and they took it how one would expect. He had to explain that it was the main factor in Jordan wanting to leave. The question of Alaska was already on the boys' minds before Jordan got diagnosed, but it was after that instance, when the choice was finally set in stone and Jordan truly cooked up the plan.

Erik, Dak, and Brandon felt a strong mix of both anger and melancholy: anger for the fact that they may have inadvertently been harming Jordan by bringing him along; and sorrow for what had become of their best friend.

Dak was the one who immediately stepped up and demanded they return to Washington; Erik and Brandon backed up the intense recommendation.

Jordan had no choice but to open his mouth and instill in them that he regretted nothing and desired to continue on.

Besides Kyle, his position confused the group. They didn't understand why he, a young adult with a long life ahead of them, would want to risk his life before even graduating high school.

Kyle, on the other hand, did know the answer–at least so he thought. He assumed Jordan *needed* to do it just as much as him. They equally shared their hunger and lust for the wild, the unexplored, and unventured. He was as clueless as one could possibly be with whether or not Jordan would soon die (perhaps within the year), but was certain that, at the very least, his friend wanted to make the most out of the time he had left. Indeed, the way Kyle figured it, if one had a good chance of dying, which one appeared more attractive: lying around in a hospital for your remaining months, knowing full-well you may never leave, or going on a life-changing adventure—perhaps shortening your life, but knowing you made the last moments count more than anything? Kyle, for one, did not like the idea of being in hospice and regretting never having gone through with the plan they'd concocted.

There may have been a third emotion in there—another sense of anger or contention. They knew that, from that point onward, Jordan was their full responsibility and if something happened to him, they would have no choice other than to blame themselves. If something bad occurred (what exactly it'd be, they didn't want to acknowledge), they wouldn't know how to move on.

To ease their minds at least half-way, he explained how it was only stage two. It wasn't good, but not the worst, and they'd be home by the time it got to three. No one could know if he actually believed that, but it's what the rest of the group wished to hear.

All-in-all, it came down to Jordan's decision. If there was even a sliver of doubt or hesitancy in his words, they'd turn around at that hour. In certain terms and with conviction, Jordan told how they were going to make it to the falls, as a team, and he had no desire to go back.

He mentioned the rest of them wanting to get there as bad as him, and it wasn't a lie. True, they were a pack and their joint goal was hermetically sealed with passion. Not one of them felt less inclined to reach their destination than the others. It was only out of apprehension for their little friend that they questioned it.

After some debate, they agreed on continuing.

In light of it, they felt it best to, at minimum, send a letter back to their parents. It was a combination of informing them that they were safe and okay, and that Jordan came at his own free will, wanting to go just as much as them.

The latter details were the most disputed. They didn't want to cause further alarm and incite their parents to organize a military search party or something. Yet, they chose not to give any details about their whereabouts (on or in the letter), only that they were away to "see something special and would return shortly"; "shortly" being an exaggeration. Inside, they included his medical notes of that day. The only parent who wouldn't receive one was Jordan's old man. He likely didn't care, nor even knew his son had been missing for the last few months.

With nowhere else to go, still being wet, and missing a tent, they had no choice but to go to a homeless shelter. It was the last thing Kyle (yet, all of them, truly) wanted to do, but sleeping on the icy, snowy streets was no better than in the middle of the woods; perhaps worse, even, seeing as they could not have a fire.

They managed to find one on the other side of town. Evidently, the homeless population in Whitehorse was small, as they easily attained beds.

As Kyle lay in his cot, he felt sour in his stomach. Part of it was due to Jordan and his continual inauspicious feelings of him recovering, while also contemplating utter disdain for where they were. In a way, according to him, they were "breaking the rules" of their adventure by being at the shelter (or even the city, for that matter), and getting sidetracked from their ultimate purpose of becoming undomesticated and returning to ancestral origins. He had to relent, however, and admit to himself that they couldn't have hoped to go on without giving in just a little and suckling off the teat of civilization momentarily. Were they now wild? Sure, he thought. Feral? Maybe. Self-reliant? Not as much as he wanted to be. To him, they'd be gone by morning with hope, but for the moment, he'd enjoy a warm, comfortable, humane bed.

When morning arrived, the conversation of what to do next was the first talk after waking. The matter of a tent and other miscellaneous resources was still up for assessment. They still had some money on hand, but not much.

Jordan was yet out of bed, and, at first, a consensus between the others was made that all their change would go towards a tent, until Brandon brought up a motel. Obviously, the boys found the idea stupid, but when he explained that Jordan should have a nice place to stay for a night and day with a good, hardy breakfast, ponderance arose. It'd be a fine surprise. Indeed, sorrow and guilt for Jordan was rife and on their minds. Indeed, he needed something special, for how long they'd be away from people from that point, no one could know. They'd still have money left over–but not enough for a tent. Brandon simply said, "I'll work something out.".

Once Jordan got up, the group walked around the city until they found a fairly cheap motel. Jordan was clueless that it was largely for him. Before entering the room, Brandon said he'd be leaving to the store. They entrusted him with the last of their dollars and told him to only get useful supplies.

Though old and not in the best condition, they found the room utterly delightful. It was warm, had two beds, a shower, a bathroom, and even a small television. Sincerely, they could not have asked for more.

Taking showers and watching toons after months in complete isolation, feasting off bugs, and having no toilet, was indescribable. The boys, though wanting to leave and separate themselves from it so as not to get too attached, relished in the lavishness and gained a greater appreciation for normal human life. They'd never take showers, heaters, or fresh water for granted ever again.

Brandon came back about an hour later. He walked in with stuff they did desperately need: lighters (which they truly loved), flashlight batteries, rope, more fishing line, water purifying tablets, nuts, and, interestingly, a cake.

The boys were thrilled that he bought significant items, but didn't understand the cake.

Likely, they would have been upset, if not for him saying it was for Jordan—which they all came to accept and admire.

It seemed that Brandon, who had always been extremely wild, careless, inattentive, and a half-witted slacker, was becoming mature and considerate. Indeed, that change appeared in all of them. With their reliance on each other came gratitude and respect for one another: more than they ever had and stronger than any group of best friends. Truly, it made them more respectable period and developed. Would they excel in man's real world and perform their expectations? Perhaps not; or, at least, never again want to, but they had at least come of age a little and blossomed into strong, upright young men.

It certainly made Jordan feel better: celebrating not his birthday, not Christmas, but his life alone. The kid deserved it. No matter how angsty Kyle felt towards his own life and situation(s), Jordan's was exponentially worse, and it had honestly been changing Kyle, just as well as the other boys. Jordan was progressively altering him, showing Kyle that things could be much, much worse, and he needed to show admiration for even the smallest hints of goodness and pleasure he experienced.

They spent the remainder of the night stuffing their faces with cake and goods, and watching black and white cartoons. It was a taste of their own past (yet, now foreign) world and, at least for a night, they'd find comfort—even nostalgia—in it.

Brandon got up before the rest around 5:00 AM the next morning and quietly left the room, making sure to turn the handle before closing the door. He went on his way back to the store and, after pretending to browse for awhile, took up a tent and a few cartons of cigarettes. Having no money, he casually and calmly walked through the exit, where a clerk swiftly began to yell and run after him.

Brandon, with his legs like Atlas's, easily outran him and the clerk was left cursing and shouting him out.

Brandon felt manic. He thought he was doing great, considerate deeds for the boys and would make all their lives easier. The boys looked perplexed as he walked through the door. When Brandon refused to explain how he'd gotten them, they immediately knew the truth.

It would have seemed that he was becoming quite the kleptomaniac, and none of the boys liked it. Albeit happy to finally have the means to continue on, they gave him a harsh scold: forcing him to promise to never steal again.

He agreed to the terms. He likely did feel a deal of remorse and shame, but again, despite growing, he still had his impulsive instincts (though small), and had a difficult time keeping his urges at bay; especially when he wished to do his friends a solid. Truly, the boys couldn't help but get grins once seeing the holy nicotine sticks.

Having until the early evening before they had to vacate the motel, Kyle decided to explore the town a bit, whilst the others wished to eat and watch the news. Being there, as it was, was not ideal, but far greater was wandering about the city than laying around in a confined cell that was a motel room. No, he could no longer be caged, and staying more than a mere few hours in even an unassuming bedroom was too much of a jail sentence.

He had no destination in mind but, unbeknownst to the others, he had a little money on his person. He chose to keep it to himself and use it only for emergencies, if he could. Hence, he didn't intend on buying anything; but, seeing as they acquired all the provisions they needed (partially through stealing), he could have a little fun with it.

After a short while, he got a glimpse of a small carnival going on in full-swing downtown. He thought it was odd–seeing as it was Winter time, but nevertheless wanted to see the festivities. For all he knew, they'd forsake man entirely for yet another couple of months at least.

It was undeniably a beautiful scene once he entered. As one would expect, food vendors, silly, hard-to-win games, rides, and mini shops littered the grounds. Scarcely an attractive setting, if not for the constant drizzling of snow and Christmas lights still hung up around every structure.

Truth be told (in his eyes), a day of fun and amusement could do him well 'til the fierce, uncultivated, and inhospitable wild welcomed him in once more.

He roamed the snowy streets, eyeing what caught his fancy until he chose to play a ring-toss game. In front of him stood a girl appearing around his age, failing to make any of the shots. After losing the game, she turned to him unexpectedly, asking if it would be alright if she went again. Of course, Kyle said yes.

In terms of appearance, "apple of Kyle's eye" was a good description of her. She had a tender and attractive disposition, rosy cheeks from the cold, light brown hair, and glasses. Of course, he could never tell such a beautiful girl to "get lost" and move for his turn—not that he would anyway to anyone.

Again, she began to fail in making the rings, and he was inwardly rooting her one. Ultimately, the game ended once again, and she was left empty-handed–both with a prize and change. Being the straight, polite, and gentleman he was (and with only they in line), Kyle offered to buy her the next game.

She naturally found it very sweet and thanked him. Again, he rooted for her, and, at the last second, she won; being rewarded a stuffed teddy bear.

At last it was Kyle's turn, but instead of walking away, she continued to stand next to him. Being one of the slyest games, he ended up losing, himself. Afterwards, she walked up to him and gave her appreciation, even calling it charming. She offered him walking with her, after both discovering they were alone. Of course, he accepted.

She introduced herself as Jennifer. She had graduated the year before (being 19), and attended Whitehorse's small community college for journalism.

It was funny how, like Dak with Violet, he was speaking (truly flirting) to a girl older than himself; but a year's difference meant nothing. They may as well have been best friends since elementary school, in terms of how long and easily they got together. Their shared interest in the natural world–free of all human ills and errs–was something exemplary.

Kyle had grown up in a fairly small city; while she, although in a far larger one, was more immersed in the wilderness and woodlands.

Jennifer resided with her roommates on the outskirts of town in a small cabin-of-sorts situated right into the *foreign* tree growth that outlined the city. Her dream was to be a reporter/journalist for a small outdoorsy town in the middle of the Cascades or Alaska, ironically. Naturally, let alone physically (which he was), Kyle felt cosmic attraction to her right from the start.

Perhaps it was not proper to call it "love" quite yet, but if the boy were to love anything besides the wild, it would've been her as they walked for hours on end, eating kettle corn and drinking hot chocolate.

He related his story to her, progressively with more detail, seemingly not caring whatsoever of her opinions. She was, indeed, extremely impressed and charmed. It was as if they were both jealous of each other. She longed to be a fierce and determined missionary for herself–to make a pilgrimage into the ungodly, desolate (yet most fruitful) lands free of man, where she could escape all worries about schools and careers.

As opposed, Kyle *did* want the same for the rest of his years, but was exceedingly fond of the "working in the woods" idea. He'd be removed from greater society, yet make a steady living where he was located and allowed to share other people's wild lives in his newspaper. It was a sweet and appealing thought.

As much as she commended and applauded him for what he was undertaking, she couldn't fathom why he'd leave both school and his good, apparently nurturing parents for such a long trip at that moment. In a way–though she kept it to herself–she felt a tad bit of disapproval and disfavor. She had his same goal, but wouldn't "escape" at such an inopportune time–essentially throwing his life away without getting a high school diploma: if he ended up dropping out.

Upon inquiring further, he began to stretch the truth and place all the reasoning on Jordan with his disease. It may have been a little selfish to do that, seeing as Kyle wanted to go more than anyone (save Jordan), while the rest also had inclinations. He figured that by blaming the hell that is cancer, she'd be more sympathetic–which did seem to work. But, she could see right through it and knew Kyle had great influence, but her opinion was fairly indifferent.

She was college educated, and well-knew that five boys wouldn't do an extremely daring, grueling adventure as that just for one of them solely, and Kyle ultimately admitted that that was true.

The snow began to fall even heavier at that point and the bulbs of the sea of Christmas lights were but giant, blurry orbs of various glowing colors.

It was then that Jennifer proposed leaving. It honestly made him forlorn. He got along with her extraordinarily well and regretted that they'd be leaving soon. To his surprise, however, she invited him to stay the night.

Despite being excited at the invitation, he felt he had to decline because of his other pals, for none of them could stay in the motel again.

Again, further to his surprise she said they could stay as well; though, not having nearly enough room, they could build snow caves in the yards.

Needless to say, Kyle was thrilled. They would have been either doing that already or sleeping in a homeless shelter (which was likely already filled).

He accepted, growing even fonder and lustful of her.

They two drove in her car to the motel, where they met the pals and she introduced herself. Kyle became slightly P.O.'d catching sight of Brandon presumably flirting with her, as well. No matter, she didn't seem to reciprocate it, showing her greatest liking to only Kyle.

They were all more than willing to stay another night in Whitehorse. Originally, Kyle was not, but he couldn't help but stay around the beautiful young lady.

They found her humble home most excellent. It fit their cherished narrative of the uninhabited, wild forest manifest destiny well. It was an old-looking wooden cabin, as she said; very cozy and welcoming.

Her roommates were all either out and about or sound asleep, leaving just them. She fixed them some sausages (the taste, amazing) and hot chocolate while they sat around the fireplace.

After a while, at even the boys' insistence, they went out and, under the lit porchlight, built snow caves. Kyle on the other hand, was offered to stay in with her; but the rest weren't jealous. They were happy to have another place to stay, as it was. Feeling woeful for Jordan, she let him stay in her bed while Kyle and her remained in the living room.

Sitting pleasurably on the couch together under the dim, flashy orange light, Kyle and Jennifer shared a bottle of wine while listening to "You Made Me Love You", by Helen Forrest, and various songs by Orrin Tucker and Carroll Gibbons on the record player.

Indeed, it seemed they were almost falling for each other, though only being acquainted for five hours or so. Their personalities were unnaturally similar and with the comfort between the two, one could have easily mistaken them for siblings or lifelong friends.

Being the crazy and passionate teenagers they were while away from their parents, and unorthodox in all mannerisms, they began kissing lying together for the remaining night, until they softly fell asleep as the trumpet orchestras and springy voice of Debroy Somers played in the background. An empty merlot bottle lay sideways on the ground as Kyle's arm was wrapped behind her neck in unconditional warmth. It was a merry and sunny day in the dreary blizzard.

Chapter 12

Moose Tracks

It was in the early morning before the cocks cawed that Jennifer and Kyle were awoken by one of her roommates, Marylin, who was not happy with his stay and insinuated that he leave. Jennifer told him not to worry, explaining that she came from a very traditional family (as most), and wasn't allowed to have boys over, according to her parents. At any rate, however, since they were up, Jennifer asked if he'd like to go to a cafe downtown. He was more than happy to follow. Meanwhile, the rest of the boys continued to sleep coldly in the quasi-backyard, unbeknownst to Maryylin.

It was a tad embarrassing, as Kyle sat at the shop's table and awaited Jennifer's return with coffee. He was more than aware that it should have been him buying the drinks, not her;

but, he knew she likely understood where he was coming from, and it didn't appear to bother her–despite not being gentleman-like.

As he sat and dazed out the window, he couldn't help but look inwardly. The smell of french toast and bacon, the warmth of the cafe, and the laughing about him: he'd taken it all for granted and never would have enjoyed it as much as that moment.

That's not to say he regretted the trip, nor didn't wish to continue on. No, not at all. The fiery passion of leaving again was burning through his chest. He needed to be back into the woods; the one, most truest place he belonged.

It was odd. In a sense, he was appreciative of the old, *foreign* things like coffee and french toast, but wanted to run away from it even more than before. The wild took something from him (as did he with it), and he was connected via soul to the mountains and streams. At that point, it was mostly Jennifer, which he found odd.

He thought little concerning it, but, if perhaps she asked him to stay with her, his lust or romantic love (whichever of the two) would overpower him and even disillusion him from his task. She, out of anyone, could hold him back from his adventure, and he'd do it at his own will.

Shortly thereafter, she approached with a black coffee–his favorite. She held a part-time job there and Kyle couldn't help but hear giggles coming from the otherside of the counter from other young adult/teenage girls who were friends of Jennifer.

The subject of Alaska again came up; not because there was nothing else to talk about, but because his story centered so tightly around it.

She longed for Kyle to stay (and maybe he even did), but knew it wasn't an option. All that he could do was promise his return.

She eventually brought up–to his complete bewilderment–the idea of her joining.

He couldn't fathom why she'd say that. He was equally (or more) fond of her, but didn't want her to throw her life away when she had so much going for her.

"You know that sounds hypocritical, right?" She laughed.

Kyle tried, with a cat holding onto his tongue, to rationalize why it was okay for him to leave school and his parents, but not her, who was free and only in college, able to resume school anytime.

"I know you think I have a good thing going," she said, "but college doesn't quite feel right for me. I could land a small job at a local newspaper without finishing a degree, or take an internship to get my foot in the door. I don't have to work for the New York Times."

Kyle didn't know what to feel nor think. Somehow he both agreed and disagreed with her. It meant the world if she came along, but then Jordan and the rest of his pals popped into his mind. The trip was for Jordan, and Kyle may as well have been his brother. If Jennifer came, the attention would be most on her, and the boys would get sidetracked. The outcome would be similar to Violet and Dak; where Kyle had to focus on his friends, and couldn't afford to ignore them. The trip was about love—that was for sure; but not the kind between a boy and a girl. Kyle was the de facto leader and the rest were his responsibility.

After explaining why they had to be his main focus, she understood, with his promise, that he'd return to Whitehorse after finishing high school.

Being the altruistic person she was, she ended up driving him to the local foodbank afterwards. She originally offered to buy him better groceries, but he was too humble to let her give up more money in his name.

In spite of it, they managed to get bags upon bags of good, appetizing (albeit expired) food that he'd return to the sure delight of the others.

There was a unanimous decision between the boys that they wished to go back into the woods that day. As much as Kyle agreed, he couldn't help but feel disappointment. Yet,

Jennifer didn't have school for another two days, so she would stay and keep them company until then, when they'd truly head back into the *unknown.*

Before they drove off into the woods, she provided them with a fair-sized sled they could use from then on. They felt stupid for not thinking of such an indispensable item. Dragging supplies was infinitely better than doddering along in deep snow with them on their backs.

They ended up on the far outskirts of the town, but still within a day's walking distance. Jennifer had brought her own Winter wear and would stay with them through the night. Second to being in love with Kyle (if one could say that), she was fascinated by the boys; perhaps there was even a seed of jealousy. As much as she wanted to travel with them and prove Kyle's mind wrong, she knew she'd have to stay, at least for a little while until the proper affairs were in order.

They spent the remaining day making snow caves. The age of using the tent was behind them, and it'd be saved for emergencies or when they were too pressed on time. Caves, although difficult and time-consuming to build, were far warmer than a tent. There were drawbacks to each, but, in the climate and time of year, *heat* was the most sacred comfort and commodity.

It was in the afternoon when they finished and Kyle instructed them to find stringy branches. After doing so, he took a large metal pot which he asked Jennifer to bring and started to boil the wood in snow melt. Once they'd become softened and bendable, he showed them how to make snowshoes with them and larger, solid branches, with duct tape.

Mostly, it was a necessity, but a part of him wanted to "show off" to Jennifer his survival knowledge he'd learned in the Scouts.

It proved exceedingly successful and, despite then being out of duct tape, they could freely and easily walk upon the snow that had originally been up to their waists.

Dak and Erik were in the process of making a fire, when, loudly, Brandon came running down a hill, shouting that he'd seen a moose. As he hurriedly grabbed his bow and arrow, Kyle only rolled his eyes and continued to help Dak with the fire.

It got completely silent throughout the whole of the forest until, ten minutes later, Brandon began screaming, "I got it!", over and over again.

Immediately, Erik and Brandon went running up the hill, but Kyle remained unconvinced–believing it was one of his pal's stupid pranks. Yet, after exclaiming that Kyle should go up and help them, he did in fact see a dead moose in the distance. He couldn't utterly believe his eyes. Brandon had miraculously stuck him square in the heart, swiftly taking him down in an instant.

In all honesty, as much as Kyle was excited, it made him sad seeing the poor beast, and he turned his head from it, questioning what Thureau would do. He knew it was uncivilized–the exalted wild, natural thing to do; but was right?

It took all of the three boys' strength even to simply get it halfway on the sled, but, slowly but surely, they got it down the hill.

At that point, Jordan had finished making a fire himself, and the elation they felt cannot be described in words. They had taken down one of nature's ultimate animals: all that was left was a bear.

Without any pause, they quickly got to work cleaning and gutting it. They had to drag the innards as far away from camp as possibly to ensure no bears/mountain lions came to dig around and enter their vicinity. As they were doing so, Jordan collapsed while standing, complaining of excruciating abdominal pain.

The boys quickly jumped to their feet and wrapped him in two sleeping bags. He took it well, saying he was alright and needed to rest–even joking that he wished for some alcohol (if he could actually have it). They laid him beside the fire, gave him water and a smoke, while

Jennifer rested beside him to redden his blue lips with warmth.

Of course, he couldn't help but jest through the pain that Kyle's girlfriend was "snuggling" with him–even though that wasn't the case.

Kyle said little, not wanting to make known his worry and upset Jordan. He began to feel extreme guilt and shame, as though he was bringing the suffering on his best friend by forcing them to keep going.

They were a weak shy of no longer recognizing Jordan–but rather seeing a mere pale skeleton.

Kyle couldn't help but get a lump in his throat. He was finally becoming aware that his initial thought of, "nature will cure him; the fresh air of the forest would heal and provide the greatest strength" was not only ignorant, but stupidly selfish. Guilt was the only word on his mind, and he questioned telling them to return to Whitehorse and call their parents.

Later that night, they slept softly and pleasantly beneath the ground in their caves. Kyle was forced to climb out at midnight to pee: a struggle to not have it collapse.

He found himself in the still, windless, and silent, pitch-black night. It was indeed eerie, and the boy, for the first time in awhile (maybe at all), sensed fear. The woods are a frightening place at midnight with no light source, and for whatever reason, he hadn't come to accept that during their whole journey. It made him realize that he still wasn't as undomesticated as he wanted to be. In spite of his Eagle accolade and being a self-proposed woodsman, there were still *foreign* experiences; in this case, the fear of darkness.

He had walked about six feet from his hole, so as not to pee directly in the middle of them, but not to walk too far. On his way back, he suddenly sunk into the snow in an instant—hearing a faint cry as it happened.

"Help!" Shouted Erik beneath him, buried somewhere near him in the three feet of snow.

In what seemed as only seconds, everyone came out with their flashlights and scrambled over to Kyle. Right away, they knew what happened.

Together, they frantically started to remove piles of snow, no longer being able to hear Erik. By the time they saw his legs, they dragged him as a scared horse would a carriage.

Erik lay motionless and unconscious. Without thinking, Brandon threw his palms on the chest of his bud and began CPR, while Dak removed snow from inside his mouth. Kyle could only watch, terrified.

After six compressions, Erik's eyes finally opened while he took a deep gasp.

"What the hell, Kyle!" Exclaimed Brandon.

The perpetrator boy apologized profusely, while Brandon berated him for not using a flashlight.

Finally, Janet rushed over and broke up the blaming shouting match between the group.

"It's okay! He's awake and it's fine now." She said, with her graceful and tender voice.

"I'm sorry, man." Said Kyle, bending down and lifting Erik up. "Really, I mean it. I didn't see a hole around me."

"It's okay, man." Erik said while catching his breath. "Just set up the tent for me. I'm not sleeping underground again."

As Kyle did so, the others accepted that it was simply an accident and, as long as Erik was okay, likewise were they.

Chapter 13

A Belated Holiday

The group awoke abnormally early in the morning, with Kyle (presumably the first, as usual) being surprised to find Jennifer up before him, having already made a fire. She truly did embody the untamed, mysterious spirit of the woods, just as Kyle did.

The other boys went straight away to preparing the moose. It was a massive risk leaving it out all night, and they couldn't afford to do it again. Regardless, they had to split it up before they made their way back through the trails.

To great vexation, it was frozen solid and they had to lean it against the fire as much as possible. After nearly six, boring and irritating hours, it was thawed enough to skin and filet.

While Brandon took charge of working on it–having great pride over his kill, Kyle and Dak took the skin, tied it tightly spread across a wooden frame of branches, and scraped the fat off of it with a buck knife. They then propped it up quite high over the fire to let it dry.

At the same time, Erik also made a frame-of-sorts out of logs, and put it into the smokey air, laying large strips of meat on it to smoke.

As much as Kyle loved it, equally were his feelings of disgust. He hated killing or handling anything dead, but embraced the *survival of the fittest* mindset with open arms. The contradicting thoughts confused him, and out of that confusion came annoyance and anger. He still hadn't entirely found himself, yet continued to fool himself into thinking he had.

The entire day was composed of eating moose steak and readying themselves for the next day: the day when their awaited, craved adventure resumed.

Again, they had to force Jordan to eat, but feasting off of the sweets and baked goods Jennifer brought, it wasn't too difficult.

As evening fell and the sky began to glow with falling, heavy snow, the coats were finally read; just in time, they thought. They cut it in such a way so as to make two kinds of tunics, using very thin strips of the hide to make rope/string.

One was given to Brandon (who deserved it), and another to Jordan (who needed it). The boys just stared at them as they tried it on, commenting how ugly and sloppy they were, but they were insulated and kept heat in. That's all that mattered.

Directly following that was likely the best night of their journey so far. It was decided that they'd celebrate a belated Christmas. It was far past, but long overdue, and with the newfound supplies they finally had and amidst the stormy weather, the setting was most fitting. Getting into the spirit was easy.

As the sun set, Jennifer brought out some chocolate and popcorn kernels, which she said to pop with the moose fat. Quite smart, thought Kyle.

To everyone's elation, Jennifer's radio still worked in her car. Their meager, cheap, portable radio had died long ago, and they were thrilled to hear the soothing, yet inspiring, sounds of Glenn Miller coming out of her open windows.

As they sat around and joked about past Christmases, there was a sense among them of melancholy and sentimentalism–maybe even forlornness. It was obvious that, despite everyone being where they wanted to be at that time in their lives, they missed their families. No other person their age could do what they were doing and not have at least some semblance of homesickness. The mood did noticeably change as this occurred. What was originally stupid, funny stories of the holidays, morphed into good memories and ones they longed to relive.

In the middle of this, two glowing, fluorescent eyes were noticed looking at them from a way in the dark trees. It seemed to roam back and forth towards them in dead silence until they could finally make out that it was a wolf.

As dangerous as it would normally seem, it didn't appear threatening in the slightest, in spite of its large figure. Its tongue was slightly sticking out and it smiled a little.

For some reason, they didn't bother to chase it away or yell at it. Brandon and Kyle grabbed their long knives as it approached, but it cautiously and harmlessly came up to them and snagged a piece of meat off of the hot rocks.

The boys couldn't help but laugh and Dak, with everyone's reluctance, even began petting it. After giving it another piece of undesired flesh, it even sat and just looked at them.

No one could believe such a savage and feral creature would be so calm around humans. It was a nice form of Christmas gift: a new pup.

As they resumed telling stupid stories and sipping whiskey, Kyle and Jennifer snuck a kiss after he handed her an arrowhead carved out of glass. It came from the melted sand underneath their fire on the beach, and he joked how difficult and time consuming it was to cut such fragile material precisely.

Again, Jennifer brought up joining them, but Kyle couldn't let himself budge. He needed to take care of his pals and didn't want her to leave all the good things she had going. He himself was aware of how selfish he was for saying that, but knew it was the truth. He could always finish high school, but college was far more important.

They promised one another that once Kyle graduated, they could stay together up North and live their lives how they dreamt of doing it. They could have their own homestead in the woods, free of all men, and live off the land. It was an attractive idea indeed.

She considered that he may have been right as she named off some of the stuff she needed to do and objectives her parents supported. As she pointed out a few, it made Kyle self-reflect. The thought arose how there were some existing responsibilities which he couldn't run from—no matter how far away into the forest. Did he have an obligation to put his parents' minds at ease and let them love him, even if he didn't think they ever would the way he wanted? Was it a moral duty to finish his education and make a living or name for himself as a respectable, upright man in society? He couldn't give a hard *no*, nor outright dismiss the notions as ludicrous; there was at least a little truth in them.

He was estranged from his contemporaries and his family (most especially), but he could never utterly or eternally forsake them. And still, did he want to be known as a dropout, a drifter, bum?

It was the same for the rest of them, he thought. Brandon, Jordan, Erik, Dak: they wanted to be where they were, they wanted to escape life, but each of them had a role to play in society. At the very least, they had a responsibility to not let others worry and to be with their families.

They were their own family at that point, he thought, and that was (if anything) a fact. Regardless of when they made it back to Washington, they'd always be brothers of the highest degree and never separate. He knew, however, that their trip couldn't last forever.

His rightful, destined place on Earth was in the woods, but that didn't mean he had to forget people altogether. He could make money off the land—run a farm, or, as before, become a forester. He could still be a straight citizen.

Indeed, fending for oneself and surviving with only one's wits and will is both noble and admirable, but humans are inherently social animals. Would he feel the same about everything if his friends weren't there?

"Nothing ventured, nothing gained", was always his saying, but he retracted it. *Nothing appreciated, nothing loved, nothing worth living for*, was the more proper idiom.

Chapter 14

Never Criminals

To Kyle's disappointment, Jennifer departed the next morning. They swore to meet again, hopefully soon, and wished one another good luck with their lives until that point.

She told them to follow the Prince river. It flowed North and animal trails ran along most of it. It was still a long trek, but the River would give them a near-straight shot to Fairbanks.

As he threw on his pack with refreshed shoulders, he watched her enter the vehicle and slowly drive away while waving at him. It made him sorrowful, even lonesome, despite knowing her only a few days. He understood the pain Dak felt when he met Violet, but the connection between himself and Jennifer was far more burning and intense. Dak was just desperate, he thought, but Kyle and Jennifer seemed bonded by a strange, eluding spark. He knew they'd meet again.

The daily routine from that point on was about the same as it had been originally, but, for a certain reason they couldn't put their fingers on, they had a noticeable increase of morale after Whitehorse. It may have had to do with another rush of eagerness post leaving society once more. Coupled with a good break, their spirits were high and the motivation to make it to the falls and see the Northern lights was greater than it had ever been.

After four days, it was all the boys–not just Kyle–who felt that they were *true* men: men of ruggedness, muscle, perseverance, and will. They were not merely one with nature, but conquerors of the wild, the merciless and uncontrollable. They were the resilient, robust forerunners of modern, weak humans who knew nothing of their roots. Whether or not they made it to Bilorid or not didn't even matter as much at that point. One of their predominant purposes was to test and free themselves of man's dependance, and that they had already done with success. All-in-all, they had journeyed around 1,900 miles; there should have been no person questioning their determination and unwavering resoluteness.

They came upon a field one evening and were awestruck to find a horde of wild turkeys. Without any hesitation, and already fueled with elating adrenaline, Brandon nocked arrow after arrow on his meek, derelict bow.

They ended up slaying five good-sized ones, slinging them over their backs until they could cook them in the evening. Between the moose meat and turkey, they ironically began to worry that they had too much food to carry. They spent the following two days smoking them as best as they could, making lighter, more easily carryable jerky cured with salt and garlic seasonings they nabbed off of Jennifer.

The weight situation was worse than they ever thought it would be. Jordan's pack was essentially empty, hardly being able to carry the pack itself, so the others divvy upped his supplies amongst themselves. Per person, the average backpack was around 65 pounds; it was no wonder their shoulders were in constant pain.

Indeed, despite their exemplary second wind, they weren't making the best time because of the poor kid. They had to stop progressively more frequently–about every fifteen minutes for a few moments of his rest. Nevertheless, they often knocked out 15-20 miles of trail each day.

One morning, they stumbled upon a dirt backroad which led straight to a beautiful cabin. It looked empty with no cars, people, and lights off. They assumed it to be a vacation home (being so far removed from any towns), and it was then that Erik proposed stealing supplies from it.

Immediately, all the boys were fervently against the idea, saying they weren't criminals, until Brandon started to change his mind and chimed in. He said how he'd already stolen stuff before in Whitehorse and wasn't ashamed to just take some candles, lighters, matches, and canned goods.

"I'll do it if you guys don't want to." He said.

The group looked at each other.

"It's not a good idea, Brandon." Kyle said, with a pondering face.

"Look at Jordan." Brandon commented. "He needs something to eat other than meat and could use a better blanket. You think they need those more than a kid with cancer? There's probably painkillers in there."

Kyle and the rest couldn't deny that he was right. The owners could afford some basic necessities, and Jordan couldn't endure going without them.

It took a good deal of persuasion and, although they were all adamant before and still didn't like it, they gave in under the stipulation that they only take what they need and nothing more.

They waited back behind the trees while Brandon went up first to scout out the place. He knocked on the door as a harmless pedestrian and, when no one responded, went to the windows and peered in.

After seeing no sign of people or dogs, he waved for them to come over.

Brandon decided to break a window, attempting to do as little damage to the home as he could. Their goal was to take as little supplies as possible, hoping the owners wouldn't even notice an absence of belongings.

To their excitement, they found the pantries full, with packets upon packets of dried rice and pasta meals. They had plenty of calories and were as light as cloth. Scattered on the tables were candles and lighters inside drawers. As they hoped, a wool blanket lay on the couch, folded neatly. At that point, Kyle was ready to leave, explaining that they had enough. It was then that he saw Dak pulling an old fashioned revolver out of a gun case.

They all debated whether or not they should take it. Truth be told, none of them were against the idea; rather sympathetic to the owners, as the piece was surely expensive. Kyle protested, but his confliction again subsided, and he allowed it.

It was at that point that he saw a picture of a family resting on a china cabinet. It was the last straw and he demanded they leave, saying they had their fill. The boys agreed, hypnotized and satisfied with the revolver most.

On their way out, Erik began to brag about the gun, fondling it in his hands and pretending to shoot it. Dak criticized him, saying he was happy too but that Erik couldn't take anything earnestly, seeing as he stole it and it wasn't legitimate; it shouldn't have been a point of pride.

Brandon walked with a handful of apples in a bag (since they tend to last a long time), and Jordan, to everyone's relief, asked if he could have one. The second he bit into it, he spit it out in disgust.

"It's wax, you idiot!" He exclaimed.

The others couldn't help but laugh at the stupidity of Brandon, who was just as hysterical. He truly was a tall, dumb beast, but his heart made up for it. Notwithstanding, they could still use it: perhaps melting the wax to coat their boots or help start a fire.

The sun began to fall behind a large mountain the thick river ran across. Kyle couldn't help but admire and respect the beauty. The day had been snowy (just like every other one), but the early night sky was of a dark blue hue: the clearest it'd been for a month, and equally blue was the snow on the sprawling topography of boundless trees. They swayed in unison, back-and-forth as though they moved to a peaceful song. Even the faint silhouettes of stars made an appearance over them and gently flickered their light over the covered branches. It was, indeed, a sight to behold.

Even still, the thought of breaking into the cabin brought him shame and he attempted to shake it out of his mind. He never would have pictured himself doing it, but had to rationalize that it was for the best; it was for the wellbeing of his buddy. He could only promise himself that he'd never do it again, regardless of what his friends wanted.

He considered that he was, for a fact, becoming the leader of the group. They always took the advice of Jordan (who had the final word in affairs), but they always followed through with Kyle's suggestions. Leaving the home was a good example. It made him happy that he acted as the parent, but wanted them to be equal at the same time. Yet, it is true, that nothing in nature is wholly equal, and there must always be an alpha in animal packs.

Chapter 15

A Lengthy Stay

It was about February 27th and the snow began to increase exponentially with extreme ferociousness. It had already been bad as it was (which was expected so far Northwest), but there started to be severe and chronic blizzards nearly every day.

Indeed, it was getting to the point where the boys only cleared around six miles every morning and had to stop at about 3:00 due to the cold and darkness. Just as bad, was the fact that they rarely were able to ignite fires and if they did, they were the smallest of ones.

This continued on for roughly a week and a half before they had to take action. During that time, they couldn't kill anything (as the meat would freeze too fast), their clothes were wet without fires, snow was difficult to melt, and mild frostbite was a constant annoyance.

It was ultimately decided that they'd make a temporary shelter–for how they'd stay there, they didn't have a clue. It was a maximum, hard choice, knowing that Jordan couldn't last in his state and Bilorid would have to wait, but they simply could not progress in the weather.

It was a unanimous decision that they do it.

Shortly after the agreement, they found themselves walking along a (presumably) dirt road in a national forest upon seeing a sign. Although it was exceedingly unlikely they'd be caught at that time of year and in that climate, they desired to get out of it before making a proper shelter. The problem was, they had no idea how far into it they were, nor how much land it covered.

The consensus was that, being an official road and not a trail, it wouldn't take them too long. Their suspicions would thankfully be proven right.

Only five hours on it, they saw the dull, foggy glimpse of a man driving down it on a B-12 snow scooter. They considered hiding, but figured the man could show them how to leave without suspecting anything of their running away.

The man slowed down, stopping to speak with them and say hello, identifying himself as a park ranger.

He asked for what god-forsaking reason they were out there at that time, and they simply said they were on a trail, got lost, and desired to return home. To their relief, he explained that the road ended in about three miles, where they'd find themselves on a main highway and out of the park–the location where their "pick up" was stationed.

To their horror, the man warned them that there were vagrants running about, and that only a short ways away a "cabin had been broken into and raided". Naturally, they pretended to be shocked, and said they'd seen no one while hiking. Not raising an eyebrow, he told them to simply "keep their wits about them".

At last, two hours later, the sign saying they were exiting the protected forest came upon them only three feet away through the fog and blizzard.

Right away, they ran into the woods in excitement. The thought of having warmth was

all that was on their minds for the last (nearly)
two weeks.

Their first line of business was to scavenge for large, slender branches, and cut those which needed to be separated. It took for what seemed to be forever, but after getting a hefty pile of long ones, they formed them into two great teepees—tying the pinnacle of them tightly with rope and tape. They then cleared all the snow from the insides, and cut millions of small branches coated with pine needles and fur.

The thick needle-filled branches were layered over every square inch of the bare teepee-like structures, until the insides of them were pitch black. It was perfect.

Throughout this whole process, Kyle was the director, and did—as was custom—fill the role of leader.

The last step was to cover the entire
pyramids in snow from head to foot. Before doing
so, they laid the rain fly of the tent over one to
stop moisture from getting in. The snow would
both stabilize them and provide insulation.
Fundamentally, they were making above-ground
snow caves, but far better.

It was decided that in a few days they'd
attempt to make an igloo; but, for the moment,
their teepees were more than adequate.

In addition to these, they made a small
shelter allocated to making a fire in. With the
unforgiving wind and snow, there wasn't the
slightest possibility that they could make one
without it.

They stayed in the teepees for the rest of
the day until the morning, cramming as many

sticks as they could into it during that time, hoping they would partially dry from their body heat.

The success of the shelters was indescribable. After an hour and a half, the temperature was obviously warm within them; such was out of the question in the thin tent.

In the morning, despite the blizzard still roaring, they perceived their sticks dry enough to try to light. Carefully, they placed them in the "fire cage", shaved wax off of the "fruits", and cut off pieces of their clothes to stick in them.

After 20 tries with the lighter, a small flame began to brew and, in a couple minutes, not only did the sticks catch fire, but so did the tiny shelter as well. At once, they yelled in joy and wanted to party, but had to move quickly to throw as much wood on it as humanly possible.

In 30 minutes, they had large flames; in 70, a bonfire. The number one most imperative goal of theirs was to never let it go out.

Again, as before with civilian food, they realized just how unappreciative they had always been when it came to heat. Like primitive man, their creation of fire revolutionized their last two weeks of living.

They tried to build their igloo days onward, but failed miserably. They didn't have snow saws, and cutting blocks of dense snow with arms and knives was utterly unfeasible. No matter, they thought, the teepees were as homey as they needed.

Each day was better than the next. Each week, they managed to shoot a deer, nourishing them with protein-rich food for days on end.

Pheasants were often another commodity that abounded, giving them a variety of options.

If they wanted to, they could have spent the rest of Winter there, and the notion did cross their minds more than once. Yet, Jordan was always the conclusion. Every hour they remained in Alaska was every moment he went without medical attention. It was no longer on Kyle who ruminated over it constantly. All the boys knew it.

They ended up staying precisely two weeks, until they had to get a move on again in mid-March. At that point, the weather had gotten far better, and the yet long mileage they had left would shorten quicker than ever.

Chapter 16

The Uncle

The situation was becoming dire with Jordan–maybe even grave. His pain was slowly becoming *truly* unbearable, and the strength to merely move was waning. His fatigue was something no one in the group had ever experienced (even during the thousands of miles they walked).

Kyle was no longer concerned; no, he was finally petrified. They were in the complete middle of nowhere, far from any establishment of medical aid. They had no choice but to continue on and monitor the boy closely.

In spite of the aforementioned, Jordan never got discouraged–let alone gave up. He was a champion of not solely the wild, but of himself and condition, which he'd long ago overcome mentally. His spirits were considerably and constantly high, with his head always firmly placed on his shoulders. Candidly, one would be hard-pressed to know a man his age, doing what he was doing, in such a grim and strict place, suffering from cancer all the while, and not be moved or impressed.

He still talked and joked at every inch of the way, never overly complaining, never placing blame on others. It was strange and even baffling to Kyle how, in the face of his physical state, he stood hopeful and undeterred to get to Bilorid. It roused and influenced Kyle in a way that couldn't quite be described. He, as he had done for the majority of his life, felt exasperation towards humanity, but, Jordan was a human just like the rest of them. Could his faith really be unreservedly absent while seeing so much goodness in another, or his friend group/family at large? Surely not, and he knew it. He needed to accept it and, albeit gradually, he was starting to.

Brandon carved two long walking sticks for him, which he used to a great extent, and Dak finally offered to carry his empty pack. A kid like him never wouldn't show appreciation.

It wasn't long until they unexpectedly came upon a small town named, "Yok". None knew of it nor remembered it on the map but, after asking around and discovering it was in Alaska, they were quite happy. They were told that fairbanks wasn't far away and that most roads led to it.

Unlike Whitehorse, they had no time to dilly dally in the town and bother with supplies. They needed to get to Fairbanks as quickly as possible.

They did, in fact, catch wind of another cargo train nearby. Knowing it'd bring up suspicion if they asked officials, they questioned locals and derelicts where it was heading to. Exhilaration filled their heads when they heard it was, astonishingly, heading in the direction of Fairbanks. Needless to say, they were going to jump it.

Getting a free ride was harder than it was last time. Stopped at first, as they walked gingerly towards it, it started to move and they increased their speed.

In no time at all, it picked up its pace and they were running at full speed. At last, they got to it and Kyle hopped in a cart first. The others were having difficulties, but Erik and Dak jumped next. It was then Brandon and Jordan left. The latter boy was having immense trouble when

Brandon suddenly picked up his 105-pound body and threw him in the cart.

At this point, the train was moving faster than Brandon could sprint. There was no way he'd make it into the cart and was forced to enter one behind them. Thankfully, Dak was able to see him and knew he wasn't a goner.

The boys couldn't help but laugh–partly because they barely made it, and also because they'd be in Fairbanks soon with no effort.

The new train was far more boring and uninteresting than the first time; perhaps due to it already being experienced. They chose to sleep the rest of the day and night.

They came to their senses about 4:00 AM when the train slowed. Jubilant were they to see a large city; it was certainly Fairbanks.

Jordan shouted out the cart to Brandon that they'd get off. They had to do so before it came to a full stop, lest they get caught by engineers roaming around. At the same time, they all leaped off and were assuaged to be united with Brandon.

It was indeed a sight to behold. The biggest city any of them had ever visited was Seattle and, although not as eye-catching, the city was rather beautiful and large.

They wandered about the town in search of coinage on the streets in order to use a payphone. After an hour, they managed to get enough and looked up Jordan's uncle in the phonebook.

They debated calling him, but Jordan, never having met him, wanted to see another relative with the time he had left (which they hoped wasn't little). They promised that they wouldn't mention the cancer to him. If they did, there's no way he'd let them continue. They went too far and were too inconceivably close to Bilorid to not see it firsthand.

The call was very odd; almost awkward. The uncle was bewildered why his nephew was so far from home and without any supervision, save his friends. Jordan simply said he'd explain more once they met–if he was okay with it.

Surprisingly, he was extremely excited to meet Jordan and offered to pick them up. He was by no means fond of his alcoholic father, but held nothing against Jordan, whom he actually felt sorrow for, knowing his foster home situation and mother.

They were told to wait at a gas station and, when he pulled up in his truck, one could notice his friendly disposition. He was a semi-small man in stature–much like his nephew–and also skinny.

It was cumbersome and slightly tricky to explain just why exactly they were there but, after him giving them some smokes and driving along, they pretty much spilled the beans on everything (except the cancer, of course).

He wholeheartedly related to Jordan, not blaming him at all and actually feeling pride towards him, but freely admitted his perspective on the other boys' foolishness leaving all they had behind–including family.

They couldn't argue with him. Though determined and iron-willed, they realized they were tossing away much of their "societal" potential; it was just that they didn't mind. That's what he found most ignorant.

Regardless of that, he was obviously impressed by the group and applauded them. He was a cool man and down to Earth. He showed no filter towards insulting Jordan's old man (which the kid understood). He commented on the uselessness of him, his disregard for his own kin, and self-destructive behavior. He wasn't wrong.

They enjoyed the small things at his ranch, which he openly offered in all ways. Like in Whitehorse, showers and warm, home-cooked meals were things to be treasured; but that time, they never underestimated their value.

As Kyle let the hot water flow unto him, he noticed the blood slightly leaking from his feet. Having gotten used to it, he no longer felt pain, but his feet were, for the most part, destroyed. He had a severe case of Christmas toe, where blood was present underneath his nails, and the amount of blisters numbered more than he could count with his fingers.

He looked forward to the reprieve of finally making it to the falls and stop hiking, but he knew they'd have to return home, and just exactly how they'd do it was still a mystery. Originally (and as long as they were gone), the plan was to walk back. In Jordan's present condition, that was out of the question.

It was, nonetheless, extraordinarily special to come out spotless and slick his clean hair to the side with some grease.

After a hefty dinner of prime rib and mashed potatoes, they boys were thrilled to sleep in warm beds in the loft. Jordan, however, stayed up for who knows how long speaking to his relative in the kitchen. Kyle wondered through the night if he ended up relating his illness to him–worrying that their journey would be cut short. Fortunately, that didn't happen.

When morning came, Jordan mentioned them having to leave that day. His uncle was taken aback that they'd stay for such a short period of time, assuming they wanted a place of comfort for at least a while, but Jordan insisted that they needed to make better time.

Being generous, he offered to drive them as far as he could towards their destination, which they honestly considered, but eventually turned down. They had made it that far, they could go a little further. In their stout minds, they didn't fully succeed if they drove the rest of the way. At the very least, the complete way there from Washington had to be of their own accord, will power, and commitment.

Again, this struck him as strange, but he appreciated it anyway and indeed saw the fire in their visage.

Chapter 17

A Heavenly Place

It was odd that the uncle didn't question Jordan's appearance, they thought. The walk outside of his house was labored yet unhurried. Of course, they didn't like it, but Jordan's condition was detrimental and disastrous. His eyes and face were scarily yellow, his bones showed everywhere, and his hair was exceedingly thin. They were nearly 25 miles from Bilorid and they could afford to stroll in his name. Even if they wanted to run in their excitement (which they did), there was no way Jordan could–let alone speed walk. It appeared as though the cancer underwent an explosion over the previous weeks and the diagnosis wasn't looking promising.

The shared consensus was that they'd return to his uncle's after, spill the beans, and have him take him to a hospital. What they all knew but didn't want to pursue in their blind, enlivened passion, was that he should have been at the hospital right then and there: far long ago, in truth. Yet, they had gone so far that they couldn't help but press onwards. It was understandable, but stupid, with even Jordan feeling the same way.

Against Jordan's wishes, they laid him on the sled and drug him. He had utterly no more strength nor vigor to walk at any meaningful pace.

Unlike the entire trip and for the first *real* time, they had a heartfelt conversation, temporarily putting their thrill of making Bilorid to the side.

In one way, they were quiet knowing that they'd soon return home and the great adventure of the century (in their eyes) would come to a close. But, mostly, it was a thanksgiving to Jordan and their personal stories of how much he meant to them. The trip was indeed dedicated to him and he was the planner, but they couldn't all but help (secretly) feel that they shouldn't have traveled so far.

No matter, though, Jordan was going to see the most beautiful and striking place he ever had–no matter the menacing face of cancer. All they could do was tell him and each other that he'd overcome the disease and everything would work out–which they really did believe. There was just that final, small and short stretch of land left they needed to cover. With hopes, they'd make it by the end of the night.

Jordan mentioned that, at first, he was scared of dying, and that feeling began to evermore increase; yet knew he had little to live for between his dad and the orphanage. That was no longer the case. Neither of those things mattered. All that meant anything was his friends and all they gave up to be with him during the way. The journey–in spite of all the obstacles–was the greatest thing he'd ever accomplished and he had never been happier. He wouldn't say it, but they all knew that he was especially speaking to Kyle, whom he'd been a brother with as long as he could remember. Indeed, he was more content and at peace than was possible.

In defiance of his small, weak figure, he was truly the strongest and most mentally fit out of any of them. Their meager aching muscles and emotional challenges were nothing compared to what he went through. He possessed a higher grade of iron will than any normal, respectable man.

The whole way, they pretty much shoved food and water down his throat. He couldn't hold out *at all* if he did not consume something.

It was taking them longer than they hoped to reach their goal, but, in the face of getting dark, there was nearly a full-moon and they could see clearly the whole night.

It was around 8:00 when it happened.

After exhaustedly going up a large hill, they reached the top and overlooked a magnificent valley—the most striking and beautiful one they'd ever seen. It was, for a fact and at last, the vast Bilorid valley.

They couldn't help but cheer and jump for joy at what they were seeing. They immediately pulled Jordan to his feet to see what they had for so long sought after.

On the other side, coming off of a 300-foot shimmering cliff, was an awe-inspiring waterfall with innumerable smaller ones trickling down around it.

The snowy valley and mountains outlining it were glowing blue beneath the moon while the graceful Northern lights swayed above, creating a long green-purple ribbon from horizon to horizon.

Their hearts felt both heavy and light at the same time; heavy, with overwhelming shock that they had indeed made it, and light with peace and merry that they could overcome anything. In total, they had traveled 2,500 miles–give or take a couple hundred. Was it worth it? No one could ever tell them otherwise.

They chose to set up camp on top of the ridge and head down to explore the valley when dawn broke.

Kyle couldn't help but continue to get sidetracked by the auroras and blue landscape as he set up the tent. It was all too powerful and moving. Truth be told, if they had driven from their town to the valley in a few hours, it'd be a pleasant sight, but nowhere near as special. It was similar to walking in the desert and dying of thirst (which they literally knew the feeling of), finally reaching a lake after months upon months. Their thirst and hunger for Bilorid was more than the valley and waterfall itself. It was a thirst for something new and those memories would be ingrained in them until their deaths.

As Kyle looked up one last time to admire the scene, he caught eye of Jordan walking downhill to get the sled which they'd left behind and forgot to grab.

"I'll get it, Jordan." Kyle exclaimed.

"I just need some water in it." Replied Jordan.

Kyle stopped what he was doing to go get it for him and let him rest. Suddenly, about 200-feet away, he saw Jordan collapse on the ground. Immediately, he sprinted as fast as he could to rescue him. All the boys stood up around the fire pit and watched in fear.

Jordan found him motionless and struggling for air. Kyle propped him on his lap and could only repeat, "You're going to be okay, pal", over and over.

"I think this is it, man." Said Jordan, beginning to tear up.

"You're fine, man. You're fine. Just rest."

Jordan's breaths were getting more labored, as though he had an elephant on his chest.

"Thank you for coming, Kyle. This is how I wanted it to be."

By this time, the other boys started to run over.

Kyle couldn't help but start to cry as he saw worry in Jordan's eyes. They both knew it was Jordan's time.

"I love you, man." Said Jordan, grabbing Kyle's hand. "It's okay, I'm happy."

"You're alright."

"It's so beautiful." Said Jordan, very softly looking up. "You've always been with me, Kyle. This is how it should go."

As the auras above spewed moving light across his face, Jordan's eyes began to shut. Kyle yelled at him to stay awake and shook the poor kid as much as he could. His heart dropped into an abyss as he saw his pal's chest completely stop moving.

Kyle could only hold onto his hand with dear life, rest his head on Jordan's, and cry unashamedly.

The other boys stood around in a circle, silent, also crying and wiping their faces. Dak put his hand on Kyle's shoulder, comforting him that it wasn't his fault and it's how he wanted to depart.

"He shouldn't have come." Said Kyle.

"It was inevitable, man." Said Brandon. "He's in a better place; no longer in pain. We made his last moments count."

As Kyle remained holding him, Erik brought over a blanket to wrap him in. It was difficult, but they managed to get Jordan out of his hands and place him on the sled.

They all sat around the sled, holding their knees and forgetting the fire and their caves.

"What are we going to tell people?" Said Dak.

"The truth." Replied Erik.

"They'll understand." Kyle muttered. "We'll go into Fairbanks tomorrow."

"At least he saw it." Said Brandon with a puffy face. "He died where he wanted to be. This is better than any orphanage or hospital. He did what should have been impossible."

The boys remained fairly quiet at first, but eventually talked positive things about Jordan throughout the whole of the cold night–not bothering to sleep or eat.

When morning came, they made the decision after much debate to make a raft for him and float him down the large river below, which likely led to the ocean.

As the boys grabbed the body and went down into the valley to build one, Kyle couldn't partake. He sat on the ledge of a ridge, staring out into the bright orange land, feeling immense shame and sorrow.

His tears were exhausted and there was no way to release his melancholy anymore. He couldn't shake the feeling that Jordan may have recovered if he'd just stayed in a hospital. Why couldn't they have just waited: waited 'til after graduation, until Jordan recovered? The feeling wasn't one of stupidity anymore–it was of guilt. All he could do was remind himself that it was Jordan himself who wanted them all to journey at that moment, as though he was aware of his own mortality and wanted to depart peacefully at that exact spot. It was comforting, hoping that's what he was thinking.

He had to keep in mind that the other pals were family too. He lost one–his best relative–but the other closest people he knew were standing beside him and they'd never leave.

As he watched them cutting branches in the distance, he wiped his eyes one last time and made his way down.

They spent all day trying to make a sizable raft, decorating it with early Spring flowers and leaves. By evening, it was complete.

They gently laid it on the water and strapped the body on top. Before letting it go, each of them said their thanks and goodbyes to him. As auroras again started to shine above in clear skies, they untied the vessel and sent him gently floating onwards. After drifting too far out of sight, a pack of moose came and crossed the river not far from them, behind Jordan.

It was a proper funeral, they thought: one fit for a true, wild, outdoorsman.

They considered spending one last night in the *foreign*, but ultimately decided their journey had come to an end and they were ready to finally go home. They accomplished all that they set out to do and there was–at least for the moment–nothing else to gain from sleeping again in a tent.

Fortunately, like the night before, the moon was exceedingly bright and they could walk without flashlights.

The revelation of Jordan's death continued to hit Kyle hard, to the point where he finally needed to share his thoughts with the others. They told him no one was to blame and, again, they did the right thing. It made him feel better, knowing it wasn't his fault, and he realized he should have truly been appreciative—as he kept forgetting.

Jordan had sent them on the adventure of a lifetime and allowed Kyle's dreamt escape from society. None of what they did would have been possible, if not for Jordan's planning. It was, in truth, his friend who showed him to be independent and iron-willed.

Indeed, Kyle even thought differently about society. Jordan (at least in part) restored his lost faith in humanity. He was a kid who saw good in everyone and, despite organizing the trip, didn't wish to completely abandon humanity.

He'd always been close to them, but after becoming a rightful pack, Kyle could see the good in people—especially them. The five of them weren't entirely outcast oddballs from the rest of the population; there were others like them.

Jordan's perspective on life was beautiful, and he had faith in two parts–that of people and nature, while Kyle only had the latter. Kyle's glass was half-empty and he no longer liked it. Where he was would always be his true home, but he could live being away from it for the moment. It was time to rest and return another time.

Chapter 18

A Sad Return

In the early morning, just before dawn, they arrived at the uncle's house to his surprise, waking him up out of his slumber.

They explained everything in great detail, not leaving out a bit of information. He was obviously taken far aback and couldn't believe his ears when it came to his nephew. Despite not knowing him well, he felt a great deal of sadness for the boy, and even a little anger—which was understandable, but perhaps not justified.

The first people to arrive were the police. They were asked on the call to look at Jordan's medical records to see that, in fact, he did have cancer, and the uncle could vouch for his terrible appearance.

The boys spoke to them with their heads down, but the officers weren't sure if they believed the group's story. Most wouldn't. After going into detail and the authorities calling their parents, they eventually came to believe them and let them off the hook, so long as they told where the direction of the body was going: information they freely gave.

The uncle offered to let them stay with him until the parents arrived, which the police came to accept by-and-by with deep persuasion.

Truly, the uncle knew not whether to be impressed or upset. It was a good amount of both.

Each person spoke little to their guardians (who were quick to put the phones down and immediately drive). They had no idea how to explain just how much happened and what they went through—let alone saying that they wanted to do it and didn't feel regret. It would take about three or four days driving non-stop until they could be put in their cars back home.

The feelings they all felt were convoluted and even contradictory. They had remorse for Jordan, wished to get back to society, and longed for basic pleasures it provided, yet, more powerfully, they were proud of themselves and would have done the journey a thousand times over. They feared their parents would bar them from ever seeing each other again: a great fear, so they wanted to savor the last moments together, if it came to that.

While the boys listened to the news and watched toons on the small television set, Kyle stood on the second floor deck and pondered while staring onward out the mountains.

The temperature was only five degrees but, oddly, it dawned on him that he no longer shivered. He'd grown accustomed to the chills and violent winds, and felt most comfortable in it more than even the heat of the furnace.

Shivering was for the weak-minded–the layman, he thought. He was feral and would never find an iota of menacing obstacles in the woods ever again.

The scenery he was gazing upon wouldn't be seen for awhile, if he was unfortunate, and, not having put a pen to his paper in weeks, he considered writing one final poem. He did so, and it was by far his longest.

His mind was utterly at ease and the content he felt was greater than it had ever been. They had all changed; himself and Dak especially. His self was obvious, but it was appealing to see what his friend had morphed into. Originally, he was the scared, always-nervous nerd who followed rules. That was long behind him. He conquered the wild and grew brave just as much as any of them and could hold his own when surviving.

He kept saying how, once back and after graduating, he'd move to Seattle and see Violet. Kyle was happy for him, but the thought crossed his mind that they'd never speak again, if he did so.

Four days later, Kyle's parents (the first to arrive) drove into the driveway.

The man (who was no longer a boy), was afraid to see them. He assumed his old man would bring out the belt and give him a good scorn. To his surprise, that wasn't the case.

They embraced him in the arms, exclaiming and expressing their happiness that he was safe and in good company. They were angry at what he did, but showed little of it. They had no desire to stay—or even say hi to Jordan's uncle, but to head home as quickly as possible.

It made him happy, seeing just how much they missed and cared for him. It was something he always overlooked and finally realized.

He pleaded to say goodbye and they let him for only a moment, asking little questions about why everything happened the way it did.

The boys all looked at each other awkwardly, not quite knowing how to say farewell, and truly not wanting to. All Kyle could do was hug all of them and say, "see you guys at school, I guess". He stood there, still not wanting to depart, until his father finally forced him to get a move on.

The ride was even more awkward, as Kyle looked out the window and saw the passing forest around him. It was mostly silent, but many questions arose. He was honest and related the happenings, answering all questions even if they resulted in scorn. They were indeed upset, but more thankful than anything.

After a few nights staying in motels, they arrived home. It was then that a little "celebration" of sorts took place, in which his mother made a large, extravagant meal for them. As good as the food looked, Kyle couldn't bring himself to eat much. His friends were all on his mind—especially Jordan. He was happy and ready to be back, but not wholeheartedly and fully. There was a piece of him missing; a large chunk of himself still lost somewhere in the wild woods that he couldn't get back at that time. He knew he'd never be the same (and presumably his friends also), but that was a good thing. He changed for the better.

Three days later, he attended school again after so long away. He was instructed to see his counselor before first period–never saying what happened to her. She gave him hope, saying he could still graduate, but only a little late if he took Summer classes with good grades, which he agreed upon.

He still did not have much interest in graduation, but knew it was the right and responsible thing to do. More than ever, he knew he'd learn nothing: having gained wisdom of all life's purposes in the foreign wild, but, perhaps from Jennifer, he became aware of some obligations one must fulfill. He may not have agreed with it, but he at last, at least half-respected civilization and understood that there must be some purpose and importance to their institutions.

In English, he sat beside Dak and spoke to him the entire period beneath the nose of the teacher. He too, didn't feel the same and thought school was absolutely ridiculous–a complete reversal of what he used to believe in his old life when he was a kid. He dearly wanted to see Violet, but the large city of Seattle scared him, and even he wanted to go somewhere free of people; perhaps live on a farm in Montana or the sort.

The other classes were the same: apathy and uninterest towards them. Gym was the lesser of these. Indeed, he found it somewhat funny. The jocks and athletic people there were limber and strong, but they had no idea just how sturdy and hardened his legs and shoulders had become.

Could any of them endure hiking 2,000 miles through desert and freezing, barren landscapes? Surely not, and let alone the mentality of it. Their petty, meaningless basketball and rugby games were nothing. The game of survival and finding oneself was the ultimate and only meaningful one.

The whole group sat beside one another at lunch and enjoyed laughing at the crazy stories they could already reminisce about. If they weren't able to see one another anywhere, then lunch would be the only place and that was fine with them.

Strangely and surprisingly, Lauren came up to Kyle, inquiring where Jordan was and saying she broke up with her boyfriend–likely wanting to be closer to Jordan. He was unsure whether or not to tell her the truth. To save a long discussion and making her upset, he simply said that he moved across the country. He remembered that the whistle Jordan made from an antler was still in his pocket, so he gave it to her, saying he wished for her to have it.

She was noticeably upset and disheartened, but understood. Perhaps it was wrong of Kyle, but it was for the best that she only felt that way.

Chapter 19

A Book Never Closed

Two nights after powering through school again, Kyle lay on his bed and considered once more running away–this time to see Jennifer in Whitehorse. Unlike before, he quickly banished the thought and knew it was stupid. His actions would be different from then on and, perhaps he would do it, but only after graduation. His time would come, he thought, but that wasn't the right moment.

Regardless of his personal duties, he actually thought about his blood family and what they'd think. They'd be devastated if he did so and their relationship would likely be permanently damaged; and, at any rate, he cared for them more than ever. He didn't want to hurt them anymore.

The following morning, he dressed up nicely to attend the funeral. Though they never found the body (likely making it to sea), it was just as special and a huge number of people were there—many of which were little kids from his orphanage.

To his amazement, he walked down the aisle, passing Jordan's father who asked to sit with him. It was a very strange and uncomfortable situation with the mumbling of him and odor of alcohol, but it was very evident that he was distraught.

Kyle soothed him, explaining that Jordan held nothing against him. It wasn't entirely a lie. Jordan had mentioned something along those lines in the heart of their adventure. Kyle wasn't sure if he believed him, but it must have made him feel better.

He poured himself out to Kyle saying that he killed Jordan and his former wife–not physically, but mentally, and was aware he damaged his son. It was a sober statement and admirable, but Kyle still held some ill-will against him, aware of just how much it affected his friend. Nevertheless, the conversation ended there and the mourning began.

After words from a priest, orphanage caretakers, and Brandon, it was Kyle's turn to give his condolences and resting words.

He started off saying how good and kind of a person he was–that he *was* (not may well as been) his brother. He knew Jordan in and out and never saw an ounce of hate in his body.

He then brought up what was on everyone's mind: the trip and what happened.

He never said how Jordan was the organizer, but that he wanted to go more than anyone and died in the best place he ever could have. He passed peacefully, gracefully, and lovingly. To ease their minds more, Kyle lied and said Jordan mentioned how he'd be happy dying while traveling. Assumably, most believed him.

Kyle had never been to a funeral before, so didn't know how exactly they were supposed to unfold, but he found it beautiful and consolatory for the attendees and loved ones.

Jordan's tale was over but not forgotten.

It cost an arm and leg that night, but the parents of the boys managed to let them hang out under the oaths that they never tried anything again. Brandon picked them up and they drove to the outskirts of town overlooking the valley from the top of a hill.

It was nice getting together again outside of the town, but the conversations weren't as promising in Kyle's eyes.

Big changes were occurring and each of them were planning on the upcoming adult lives.

Kyle already knew what Dak was doing but was clueless of the ambitions of the others. Kyle said his first: how he'd return North in just a few short months.

The plan wasn't to relate everyone's plans, but it sort of just came up with the talks.

Erik was going to head to North Dakoda and find a stable job there, while Brandon had already put in an application for Oregon State University.

Frankly, it made Kyle mad, but sadder more than anything. They'd all be departing ways and, for whatever reason, he was truly hoping they stay together. It was a fool's prayer and he should have known that likely wasn't going to happen.

None of it meant that they *wanted* to go different directions. Not in the slightest, but it was the way of the world and they'd have to figure out their lives. Unlike Kyle, they couldn't live their entire lives in the wilderness, as much as they wanted to.

More than anything, it made him dispirited knowing there was little chance they would see each other ever again—despite them all promising they would. They were simply unrealistic pledges ignorantly thought to always stay true.

Even Kyle couldn't deny his doubts. Even if they all stayed put in their hometown, he'd be over a thousand miles North and probably wouldn't come down. Odds-on, he'd marry Jennifer and make a living as a forester.

Notwithstanding, he was a believer in fate, and what happened of them was for the better. In any case, they'd always be brothers and be there for one another at the worst of times. He had to appreciate the time they had together–just like his saying.

He sat at his bedroom desk that night around 10:00 with a stack of papers and telephone in front of him.

He considered compiling his poems and turning them into a book. It was an exciting and ambitious idea, but again wondered if things of such personal meaning are best left to be savored in one's own mind and memory alone. Perhaps he'd write a fictitious novel based on his experiences—a book like Call of The Wild. Only time would tell.

The woods were not just a chapter of their lives, it was the personification of a book that permanently defined their lives and would always be on their healed shoulders.

Adventures could be anything, he thought. Overcoming obstacles was a journey in itself, and it didn't have to mean running away.

In the meantime of his goals, as he sat there in the light of his lamp and silence, he picked up the phone and dialed Jennifer's number.